POWER PLAY

A GRAY LADY NOVEL

ANNIE REED

ROBERT JESCHONEK

POWER PLAY
A GRAY LADY NOVEL

Published by Blastoff Books

Copyright © 2025 Robert Jeschonek
www.bobscribe.com

and Copyright © 2025 Annie Reed
www.anniereed.wordpress.com

Cover Artwork Copyright © 2025 Felipe "Philcold" Frias

Cover Design Copyright © 2025 Annie Reed

ISBN-13: 979-8-9925842-2-6

ALSO BY ANNIE REED

ALSO BY ROBERT JESCHONEK

PROLOGUE

Power.

That one word meant so many different things.

In the military, power meant physical force. Armed warships. Armed infantry. Armored warriors. Physical power that could blast anything and everything that stood in its way into oblivion. The Alliance's military machine was the strongest fighting force known to man. The protection the military provided member worlds was a large part of why the Alliance kept bringing more and more worlds into the fold.

Protection came with a price, of course, but worlds plundered by the lawless rarely took that into consideration.

For the obscenely rich, money was power. The power to buy whatever—or whoever—they wanted.

Exchequer was the very embodiment of monetary power. Exchequer was the largest financial institution in the Alliance. In a very real sense, Exchequer determined which businesses succeeded and which failed, who lived and who died. But even at the very lowest levels of society, money equated to power. Those who had it, had control. Those who didn't could *be* controlled.

For politicians, power went hand-in-hand with their hierarchy in the political machine. The higher the office, the more power the politicians wielded over their fellow citizens.

Heady stuff, political power. In Alexander Krepnick's experience, those who had it would do anything to keep it.

He was well acquainted with all the various forms of power. But he also lived by a maxim that few inside government, inside the military, or even inside Exchequer understood.

Ultimate power came from knowledge.

Krepnick had made the acquisition of knowledge his life's work. As Director of Military Intelligence, he was a master at using that knowledge not only to increase the scope and power of the Alliance, but also for his own best interests.

He knew all the dirty little secrets of the rich and famous. The politicians. The generals and admirals and regional military governors. Even the scientific community. He made it his business to acquire information about all the little backroom deals. The shortcuts taken. Bribes offered and accepted. Payoffs made in the hope that secrets would remain hidden.

He hoarded information like a miser, keeping the best tidbits solely for himself like one of the dragons in the tales from old Earth. Monstrous creatures who sat on enormous piles of gold and jewels.

Unlike fictional dragons who would fight to the death to prevent even a single piece of gold from leaving their greedy clutches, Krepnick never hesitated to use the information he collected whenever circumstances dictated. That was another maxim he lived by. Power was an illusion if the person holding it was afraid to use it.

Military Intelligence was the most feared division in the Alliance, and Krepnick was the most feared director to ever head the division precisely because he was willing to use the division's accumulated knowledge as he saw fit.

The power at his fingertips would have corrupted a lesser man. It had corrupted his predecessor, a weak and pitiful man who had devastating secrets of his own he never wanted to see the light of day.

That was the thing about secrets. A person with secrets could be manipulated.

Krepnick would never be in that position. He had no devastating secrets to uncover. No skeletons in his proverbial closet. He was a company man, and the company he served was the Alliance.

He'd risen to power through his complete, some would say ruthless, devotion to the Alliance. As soon as he realized how compromised his predecessor had been, Krepnick had forced the man to resign.

Krepnick had held his position now for nearly a quarter century. No one dared challenge him. A few had tried in the early years, but their utter defeat had become an object lesson to anyone else with thoughts of trying to usurp Krepnick's position.

He wondered if the junior officer he'd summoned to his office planned to someday step into Krepnick's place.

The man was older than Krepnick, with the beginnings of gray invading the dark hair at his temples. He was thin, as many who lived their lives on remote postings in space tended to be. But he had a certain air about him that Krepnick had come to recognize.

This was a man who thought *he* was the most important person in any room. His ego had grown large during the years he'd overseen military intelligence operations in one of the far-flung sectors in the Alliance. He appeared appropriately obsequious in Krepnick's presence, but Krepnick knew it was just an act meant to placate him.

He hadn't risen to the office of Director because his ego was so easily stroked. A lesson this junior officer would be learning shortly.

But first Krepnick would discover what information, what *secrets*, this man had failed to include in his official reports.

Krepnick kept his back to the man, leaving him to sweat in his seat at the far end of the conference table while Krepnick stood gazing out the floor-to-ceiling windows that comprised an entire wall in his office.

The office was far more spacious than Krepnick would have chosen for himself. The conference table alone sat twenty with ease, and Krepnick's desk was nearly three times as large as what was necessary to project the screens on which he did his work. But his predecessor had chosen this office, and moving to a smaller, less luxurious space would have sent the wrong message about the importance of Krepnick's position within the division.

The office had a spectacular view of the capitol city. The windows were made of clear, self-healing alloys that would repel all known energy weapons as well as projectiles and explosives. It wouldn't do to have the Director of Military Intelligence assassinated by an outside force as he gazed out over the city.

As for assassination attempts from *inside*, Krepnick had taken precautions there as well.

His office included highly classified technology keyed solely to his own biometrics. The covert tech not only afforded him a 360-degree view of his office as well as the city outside his office, but also allowed him to monitor the biometrics of everyone within his office.

Right down to their every minute physical reaction.

Increased heartrate. Increased blood pressure. The sudden tensing of muscles that might signal an assassin getting ready to attack.

The tech scanned everyone for the presence of poison on their skin or in their clothing. The tech sampled the minute cells everyone's body discarded naturally to search for pathogens carried in their bodies. It sampled the air around them to look for chemical compounds that would signal explosives were embedded in their clothing or beneath their skin.

It even scanned the chips embedded in their bodies to determine each chip's purpose and whether the original purpose had been altered.

Krepnick knew more about each person who entered his office than the person knew about themselves.

He was not a paranoid man. He was a pragmatist. A man who was as feared as Krepnick was a man with a target on his back. Only a fool would ignore that fact.

This junior officer was ambitious, but he was no assassin. He had no weapons on him. No blood-borne pathogens or fast-acting poisons. The only chip on his person that had been altered was set to surreptitiously record this meeting.

With the hope of catching Krepnick in some type of verbal trap?

Krepnick would soon disabuse the officer of any such hope.

Satisfied that the junior officer posed no immediate threat, Krepnick turned away from the windows and took his seat at the opposite end of the conference table. He triggered his own recording devices. The meeting would not be brief, but in the end Krepnick would find out what he needed to know.

He always did.

He gave the man a slight, noncommittal smile, and the man relaxed. The junior officer believed he was ready for this debriefing.

He wasn't. He just didn't know that yet.

Krepnick placed his hands on the top of the conference table. He tented his fingers and gazed at a man whose promising career was about to come to an end.

"Let's get started," Krepnick said. "Shall we?"

CHAPTER 1

Gus Light never had a honeymoon.

Augusta "Gus" Light joined the military when she'd been little more than a kid. She'd put up with all the hazing that came with not only being the only female cadet who'd applied for service with the Armor Division but also the smallest. She'd had her signature gray hair already, and her fellow cadets—all male—gave her the nickname Gray Lady to further humiliate her.

It hadn't worked.

She'd *owned* the damn nickname. She'd worked her butt off to not only qualify to wear the armor, but to beat every one of her fellow cadets in whatever training exercises the drill instructors dreamed up. She'd kicked ass at everything thrown her way, and graduated basic training at the top of her class. She was hard working, hard drinking, and just plain hard period. By the time she was assigned to the 83rd

Armor Division, the last thing on her mind had been falling in love.

Then she'd met the man who would become her son's father.

They'd both been part of the 83rd. The military sent the 83rd all over Alliance space to defend whatever remote world needed defending. They never got time off for good behavior, much less for a private vacation to a remote corner of the galaxy where they could spend entire days and nights between the sheets.

After Gus found out she was pregnant—much to both their surprise—they talked about leaving the military. Getting married. Settling down and raising their family.

That never happened.

The night their one and only son was born, his father was mortally wounded protecting a diplomatic mission from armed guerillas.

Gus left her own hospital bed to rally the remaining members of her squad. With Gus in the lead, her squad wiped out the remaining guerillas, but in the end she was forced to leave her newborn son behind on the planet where his father had died.

After her private world had fallen apart, Gus became a one-woman berserker. She'd amassed so many medals for bravery in combat that the Gray Lady of the 83rd Armor Division became a hero.

She hadn't been a hero. She'd been unhinged. Uncontrollable. Unable and unwilling to follow orders, she'd charged into every battle with not so much a death wish as an unquenchable thirst to wreak vengeance against anyone and everything that harmed the innocent.

A military psychologist would have had a field day examining her head. Not that she'd ever gone to any mandatory counseling sessions. She'd been too busy being one of the Alliance's top armor warriors, and because she was just so damn good, her commanders let her get away with it.

Then they accepted promotions based on her achievements.

Throughout it all, she'd remained deliberately unattached. She was no saint, far from it, but she never let anyone break through the shell she'd built around her heart. She never even sought out her son. He'd grown into a fine man who didn't know the Gray Lady was his mother, and she'd be damned if she'd blow apart the life he'd made for himself out of some selfish need of her own.

Her military career ended when the powers that be decided to decommission her armor. That armor was the closest thing Gus had to family. She'd tweaked it and customized it and made a million little improvements to it over the decades, and she wasn't about to let the Alliance trash it into so much garbage.

So she'd thumbed her nose at the military, liberated her armor from the scrap pile, and found an out-of-the-way space station in an out-of-the-way sector of space where she planned to drink her way through retirement and die the same way she'd lived most of her life.

Alone.

Then Mephistopheles Drake came into her life.

Drake with his laidback cowboy charm. His cinnamon gum. His antique guitar and ancient cowboy songs.

Of course, looking at it from his perspective, she'd

barreled into *his* life. She'd taken charge like she always did, and turned the relatively quiet life of a struggling smuggler upside down. She'd commandeered his ship, paid his overdue debts, and taken his ship—and Drake—into the heart of a civil war.

All to rescue her son from the latest version of the same guerillas who'd killed his father.

With a more than able assist from Drake, Gus had saved her son's life. She'd been hailed as a hero again, but this time she'd left before anyone attempted to pin a medal on her chest.

That had been the first of their many death-defying adventures.

Somewhere along the way, Drake had wormed his way into her heart, and she'd wormed her way into his.

Drake was the polar opposite of her son's father, but in the best possible way. Gus had never imagined she would fall in love again, but she had.

After their latest adventure, they were on what could only be described as a well-earned honeymoon.

Not that they were married. They hadn't even talked about the possibility. As far as Gus was concerned, she didn't need an official document to prove their devotion to each other. She was pretty sure he didn't either. They'd survived battle after battle, relying on nothing but their wits, their skills, and a grim determination not to live in a universe that didn't have the other in it. As far as she was concerned, that was more than enough proof they were meant to be together.

She sat up in bed and glanced down at Drake, snoring

away lightly after a more than strenuous workout session between the sheets.

Or in his case, beneath an honest-to-God down comforter.

They were in his cabin on his ship, the *Golden Void*. He'd furnished the otherwise spare room with not only the comforter, but real feather pillows. The pillows had fallen victim to numerous pillow fights during the course of their relationship, and then been stitched back together again—after the loser picked up all the errant feathers.

Not that either one of them ever lost. Drake just believed, like Gus did, that a little healthy competition only served to enrich a relationship between two people who'd been loners most of their lives.

One of the feathers from their latest pillow fight had landed on the comforter near Drake's face. Gus picked it up, and with one side of her mouth quirked up in a wicked grin, she brushed it beneath Drake's nose.

He swatted at his nose with one hand, but didn't quite wake up.

She adjusted the angle of the feather and this time ran the feather down his nose, from the slight frown line between his brows to the tip of his nose.

He snorted, still sleeping.

Okay, buddy. Just how badly had she worn him out?

She was about to find out.

She dropped the feather and eased her hand beneath the comforter. When she found what she was looking for, she squeezed.

Drake yelped, his eyes flying open. "Holy crap!"

Gus chuckled. "Wake you up, did I?" she asked.

He rolled over on top of her and pinned her with his weight. She could have easily toppled him off, but she liked him right where he was.

"Darlin'," he said. "You have *no* idea what you just woke up."

Oh, she had a pretty good idea.

He kissed her, and she melted against him.

For someone who'd been a warrior most of her adult life, this kind of closeness was something she never thought she'd have, much less enjoy as much as she did. Armor jocks were an odd combination of self-contained war machines and coordinated fighting units. When armor jocks got together, it was more about letting off steam than any kind of closeness. They certainly didn't cuddle.

But with Drake?

It felt right, this being part of something that was larger than herself.

They were just getting to the really good part of two becoming one when the sound of a clearing throat interrupted them.

They were, for all intents and purposes, alone on the ship. They'd *been* the only two people on the *Golden Void* for weeks now. There was only one other sentient being who could possibly be interrupting them right about now.

Bruce. The ship's AI.

Bruce had started out as the *Golden Void's* standard AI computer system. When Gus first came aboard, she renamed the system Earl after a particularly obnoxious armor jock from back in her days with the 83rd. Who wouldn't want to be able to boss around a bully who used to make your life a living hell?

Gus and Drake had later renamed the system Bruce in honor of someone who'd helped them out of a jam.

Then Bruce got an upgrade courtesy of the Fluke as a thank you for providing the unpredictable and all-powerful aliens with an entertaining gambling opportunity. The upgrade had not only supercharged Bruce's AI capabilities, it had given him a personality.

A personality that mirrored normal human emotional development.

Right about now the *Golden Void's* ship's computer was the sentient AI equivalent of a hormonal if somewhat unpredictable teenager.

Who'd just interrupted his surrogate parents having some private time in the captain's quarters.

Which he was definitely *not* supposed to do.

Gus tried to stifle a giggle at the look of pure frustration on Drake's face.

"Bruce Azazel Ozzyborne, this had better be good," Drake said to the AI.

While Gus occasionally called the AI by its full name—it had chosen its middle and last names for itself—Drake rarely did. And like any teenager whose parent calls them by their full name, Bruce knew it was in trouble.

Gus could practically hear the AI gulp.

Which was impressive since it didn't have a physical body. Other than the ship itself, of course, and one thing the *Golden Void* couldn't do was gulp.

Or be embarrassed. Bruce could do both.

"I'm not looking!" Bruce said. "Honest!"

A giggle burst through Gus's pursed lips. She couldn't help it.

At least she and Drake were both still beneath the comforter.

"Just spit it out," she said to the AI. "We got about another five minutes or so—"

"Ten," Drake said.

"—okay, make it fifteen," Gus said, wriggling beneath Drake, which produced a satisfying groan from the captain. "So tell us what's so important you felt you had to interrupt."

"In my defense," Bruce said, "you've been spending an inordinate percentage of your time in *alone* time. Which isn't really alone in the true meaning of the word, according to my re—"

"Bruce!" Gus and Drake said together.

They both burst out laughing, and this time Gus had to stifle a groan. She really, *really* wanted to finish what they'd started.

"Get to the point," Gus said when she got herself under control.

Bruce cleared its non-existent throat again, and when it spoke this time it sounded far more adult. More mechanical, which made Gus wonder if she'd hurt its feelings. She had been a little abrupt. For a good reason, but still. She had to remember that AI Bruce could be more than a little moody.

"I'm receiving an encrypted transmission," Bruce said. "Voice only, on loop. Directed to the *Golden Void*, addressed to Augusta Light."

Augusta Light?

Nobody called her Augusta.

Nobody who wasn't official.

"Point of origin?" Gus asked.

"I am unable to determine a point of origin," Bruce said.

Okay, now that sounded potentially dangerous. Bruce's Fluke-enhanced capabilities were beyond any normal AI, which meant he could track almost anything back to its source. No matter how far away it originated.

Drake shared a look of concern with Gus. "Content of message?" he asked.

Bruce was silent for a few beats. "I can't decrypt the message," he said, and now he did sound miffed. "There appears to be a code accompanying the transmission, but when I attempt to use it, nothing happens." He paused. "I even attempted to enter the code using Gus's voice." Another pause. "There's no rule against *that*."

Defensive. He was definitely getting defensive.

"You did good," Gus said, even though she'd have to talk to Bruce later and set some ground rules about when he could and couldn't imitate their voices.

"What's the code?" Gus asked.

Bruce read off an alphanumeric sequence. Gus recognized it immediately.

It was the first part of the override code for her armor.

The override code that the Alliance had installed back when her armor was first assigned to her.

The override code was a failsafe the Alliance installed in every military suit of armor. It allowed the highest echelons in the Alliance military to shut down the armor in the event an armor jock went totally rogue or the armor was captured by an enemy.

At least, that was the theory.

In practice, every armor jock futzed with the override

code enough to make the failsafe ineffective even though it was a court martial offense. Gus had certainly zapped the code on her own suit of armor. No one but no one was going to pull the plug on her armor in the middle of a firefight.

She still remembered the code though. Even all these decades later that alphanumeric sequence was burned in her brain.

This told her several things about the transmission.

It was coming from someone in the Alliance who had access to that code, which meant military. Not only military, but military *intelligence.* It had to be. The high-ranking officers in the Armor Division who'd had access to that code, decades out of date now, had all either moved up the ranks or retired. Military intelligence, however, had access to *everything.* Including those old codes.

That was bad news. She'd had run-ins with military intelligence before, and it never turned out well.

To say the least.

The encryption also told her whatever the message was, someone was being very careful about the transmission being intercepted. Even Bruce, with all his Fluke-enhanced AI capabilities, couldn't decrypt the transmission because he didn't know that it not only required the remaining alphanumeric sequence, it required a sample of her living DNA. Something that Bruce couldn't provide.

She locked eyes with Drake.

"This is serious, isn't it darlin'?" he said. "I can tell by the look on your face."

It most definitely could be.

The *Golden Void* was still in the Frontier, well beyond

Alliance space. Technically the Alliance couldn't reach them here.

But technicalities were only a minor inconvenience where military intelligence was concerned. Hell, military intelligence had sent one of their covert agents, a retired armor jock by the name of Garrison Brukowski, on a one-way mission to destroy classified military tech deep in the Frontier.

Gus had served with Brukowski in the 83rd. She'd always thought he was a promotion-seeking, self-serving jerk. Instead he'd turned out to be an honorable man dead set on completing a mission that in the end had cost him his life.

That was the thing about military intelligence. People were just pawns to be used to win whatever game the brass was playing.

Gus hated the idea of being used. She'd had enough of that when she'd been with the 83rd. Armor jocks were the epitome of pawns in vast games of chess. Nobody in command cared if they lived or died. They could always be replaced.

She supposed she could ignore the transmission. Pretend it hadn't reached her.

The problem with that was it would eat at her.

If the sender couldn't reach her, who would they contact in her place? She'd never run from a fight, and right now all her instincts were screaming at her to get ready for a big one.

She gave Drake a quick kiss. Was it serious?

"We better go find out," she said.

CHAPTER 2

"What the *skudge* kind of encryption *is* this?" asked Drake as he watched Gus prick her index finger with a medical-grade needle in sickbay.

"Very thorough." A drop of blood welled up from the tiny puncture, and Gus wiped it on a glass slide she'd pulled from a box on the stainless-steel counter. "The kind that takes nothing for granted."

"Message decryption by way of bloodletting." Drake shook his head. "It's a new one on me, that's for sure."

Clearly, it wasn't new for Gus. She'd known exactly what to do. Did military armor jocks have to do this sort of thing all the time? Gus had never said, but then again her military days were ten years in her rearview when they'd met.

Carefully, Gus placed a second slide on top of the first, then laid them on a tray under a scope on the counter. "Ready to scan when you are, Bruce."

A beam of bright light bathed the stacked slides, capturing the contents between them. Gus, meanwhile, grabbed a slim silver cylinder, six inches long, from a shelf above the counter and sprayed her finger with restorative foam.

"*Genecryption* was my next guess, you know," Bruce said over the sickbay speaker. "That the encryption matrix incorporates the structure of the recipient's DNA. I had it figured out. Just wanted to see if *you* two would understand, too."

Drake smirked at the adolescent AI's effort to take credit after failing to solve the problem itself. He wouldn't call it *cute*, exactly...but somehow, he found it reassuringly human-adjacent.

"It's pretty simple, really," said Bruce. "Once you *know* there's a genetic component, and you have the DNA and armor override code, it's just a matter of converting the gene sequence to numeric values and applying an algorithm that will sort and index..."

"Glad you can handle it." Gus winked at Drake. They'd both learned to politely cut Bruce short before he went too far down an expository rabbit hole. He was still having trouble recognizing and adjusting to certain social cues, like knowing when it was time to shut up. "How soon can you have the message contents fully decrypted?"

"Almost done," said Bruce. "Stand by."

Gus held up her hand and examined the pricked finger.

Leaning in for a closer look, Drake saw the healing foam had been fully absorbed and done its job. No more blood seeped out of that finger; the tiny wound was no longer visible at all.

"Here." Taking her hand, he softly kissed the finger. "All better now."

"Always is." Her eyes remained worried, distracted... but she smiled. "Any time, anywhere you kiss me."

"Works both ways."

He kissed her finger again, more lovingly. After spending so much time together on their "honeymoon" getaway, he felt closer to her than ever. Their relationship may have been forged and reinforced in battle, but alone time free of danger and chaos had done a lot to lift their bond to an even higher and more intimate level.

"Ding!" Bruce said after another moment's effort. "The message has been decrypted. It reads as follows—"

"Whoa!" snapped Gus. "Hold on there, Bruce! Let me see it onscreen first! On *this* screen." She pointed at a monitor angled into the stainless counter.

Angled so that she'd be the only one who could read the display.

Drake frowned. What was that all about? He respected her privacy, no question there. They'd both had long lives before they met each other, but he figured they'd shared most of the highlights with each other.

The highlights that mattered, anyway.

But she'd been worried about this message ever since Bruce had interrupted their alone time. She hadn't even taken the five minutes to finish what they'd started before donning her clothes and heading toward sickbay.

What reason might she have for concealing the contents of this one particular message from him?

She seemed to understand his concerns and nodded. "I just want to make sure there are no...surprises."

"I get it," said Drake, though what she said just made him wonder more intently what she might think she needed to hide. "No worries."

"Thanks, Cowboy."

"Here it comes," said Bruce. "Full disclosure, I *did* read the text during decryption. Impossible not to...but no spoilers, I promise."

"You're fine." Drake nodded. "We trust you."

"Thanks for that, Captain." Bruce had a smile in its voice. "I trust both of you, too."

As the monitor screen lit up with a page of text, Drake turned away, giving Gus the privacy she'd requested. Whatever was in that message, he would know it soon enough; the two of them shared pretty much everything these days, especially when it came to information that was vital to their mutual well-being.

Sure enough, she spoke up after a moment. "It's from someone in military intelligence." Her voice sounded tense. "An...acquaintance of mine from the old days."

Drake glanced over his shoulder, but her back was still turned to him. It wasn't time for a peek at the screen just yet.

"Is that a *good* thing?" he asked.

Her silence spoke volumes.

For another few moments, the only sounds came from Gus twisting the knob to scroll through the message and her fingertips tapping on the counter.

Meanwhile, Drake's imagination ran wild. Like him, Gus had had what people might call an *interesting* life. Since joining forces, she'd told him quite a few stories from her highlight reel, and aspects of her past had cropped up in their adventures. But he was sure there was plenty he didn't know about yet. What such revelations might mean to them —and even Bruce, for that matter—was enough to cause him some heartburn as he waited.

As easygoing as he tended to be, he'd come to care for her deeply. He didn't want anything to get in the way of their lives together, especially some bit of ancient history that should have remained long buried.

"Well, hell," she said finally. "So much for our honeymoon, Broken String."

Drake recognized his cue and turned around. "What is it, darlin'?"

"Tell him about the singularium," said Bruce. "And the ring ship!"

Gus rolled her eyes and shook her head. "Bruce! I thought you said there'd be no spoilers!"

"So?"

"So what you just *did* is the very *definition* of a spoiler," explained Gus. "You blurted out what I was gonna say before I could *say* it."

"Yeah, but..." Bruce made a sound like a sigh. "Sorry."

"It's okay," she said. "You didn't mean any harm, did you?"

"Absolutely not!"

"So it's okay if I continue my story?" Gus asked.

"Sure, go ahead! Just don't forget the part about..." Bruce caught himself. "Never mind."

Gus pushed back from the monitor and cleared her throat. "What he said." She looked grim. "Someone wants us to find the singularium ring ship—or what's left of it—and claim it for them."

The singularium ring ship.

Drake thought he'd never hear those words again. They'd fought a skudging *war* over that thing. Just when it looked like they might actually lose to more pirates than Drake had ever seen in one place in his entire life—pirates who'd been promised the singularium bounty of a lifetime in exchange for their services to a wannabe emperor—the ring ship had up and disappeared.

Not *exploded*. Or *imploded*. Just flat out *disappeared*.

No bounty, no pirates.

The pirates fled the scene. After Gus and a ragtag group of armor jocks captured the wannabe bad guy, Drake figured they'd left the whole mess far behind the *Void's* rear thrusters.

Now here it was rearing its ugly head again.

Drake scowled. "What in the *skudge* would make us do *that?*"

"Blackmail." Gus was dead serious when she said it. "If we don't deliver, he'll ruin a very dear friend of ours... someone who basically gave me back my life again."

"Who?" Drake could think of several people who'd helped make that possible.

"Kymmie." Gus glared. "The bastard says he'll take her down if we don't do what he says."

Skudge.

Whoever the bastard was, he knew how to get to Gus.

Kymmie had come a long way from the wet-behind-the-ears reporter who'd first interviewed Gus way back before Gus had barreled her way into Drake's life. After Gus had captured the wannabe emperor Jorritz Tor, Kymmie had brokered a deal with the Alliance that cleared all charges

Gus had racked up by using her armor in ways not autho-rized by Alliance military. Gus had been a wanted person subject to immediate arrest if she entered Alliance space, and all her assets in the Alliance, including a considerable amount of money, had been frozen. Kymmie had made all that go away.

As Gus said, she owed Kymmie her life. Gus wasn't the type of person who took that lightly.

"Would he?" asked Drake. "Could he?"

She nodded. "The answer to both questions is yes."

"Huh." Drake pulled a stick of cinnamon gum from the pocket of his red flannel shirt, peeled off the paper wrapper, and slid the gum into his mouth. "I guess you already know how I feel about this, don't 'cha?"

Gus smirked. "You wanna strap him to the engines, jump to maximum velocity, and watch the teeny, tiny bits that are left of him shoot off into the far reaches of the galaxy."

Drake grinned. "You know me so well, Gray Lady."

"It's a good plan," she told him. "But until we manage to get to this guy, I think we have to play along."

"But what he's asking isn't even possible," said Drake. "Doesn't this guy know the thing's just flat out gone?"

Gus shook her head. "He claims it's still out there. He's even given us rough coordinates of where to find it."

Drake's eyes narrowed. "That doesn't make sense."

"Tell him that."

Drake paced across sickbay, still gnawing on his gum. He didn't like how the situation was taking shape. It smelled like a setup, or at least a trap...though he couldn't quite envision what the end game might be at the moment.

The worst of it was, with Kymmie in jeopardy, they had no choice but to play along. Gus was right that she'd given her her life back. Without Kymmie, Gus would still be a fugitive, unable to enter Alliance space without fear of being apprehended and imprisoned.

Kymmie had helped them in so many other ways, too, using her position as a reporter to bring attention to their struggle. She had proven her devotion to them again and again, more than earning equal devotion from them in return.

Hanging her out to dry was *not* on the table.

The decision was made. All that remained for them to determine were the details.

"All right, then." He stopped pacing in front of Gus and gazed into her eyes. "Let's do this thing."

"Honeymoon's over," she said with regret.

He reached for her face, brushed his thumb across her cheek. "Honeymoon's not over till I *say* it's over." Then, leaning forward, he kissed her lovingly.

As their kiss continued, Bruce interrupted...reluctantly, for once. "Captain? Gus?"

They didn't answer.

Bruce made a sound like a cough. "I, uh...was just wondering..."

Gus broke the kiss. "Wondering about what, Bruce?"

Bruce hesitated, seemingly thinking something over. "The blackmailer who wrote the letter. Didn't he also say—"

"Doesn't matter," said Gus, interrupting Bruce yet again. "Nobody threatens my friends...my *family*...and gets away with it."

"But..."

Gus waved a hand at the air, a clear indication to the AI to shut up.

Bruce shut up.

She kissed Drake again, then led him out the door. He went willingly, happy to join her on another quest, another mission to defend someone who'd made a difference for them both. Loving Gus with all his heart as he did, there was simply no other choice he could make.

After the door to sickbay slid shut behind them, Bruce let out a sigh.

He knew the room was empty. With his global awareness of the ship, he knew where everyone was on the ship at every moment.

He wasn't sure why Gus—and he'd just recently started to call her Gus, which she hadn't seemed to mind—would want to keep him from asking about the rest of the encrypted message. She'd even erased it from the monitor so that the Captain couldn't read it, which seemed totally out of character for her. From what he could tell, she never kept anything from the Captain.

Bruce didn't always understand the emotions of the humans he interacted with on the *Golden Void*. He supposed that was logical since he didn't always understand his own emotional responses. Emotions were just so difficult to master! Fear was bad. But one of the worst, he was learning, was frustration. Especially when he had no one to talk to about what it felt like to be frustrated.

Was that why Gus had stopped him from talking? Had she been frustrated with him?

He was certainly frustrated now.

Frustration was what made him keep speaking to the

empty sickbay. It wasn't logical, but sometimes Bruce just needed to *vent*.

To ask a question he felt absolutely needed to be asked even when there was no one to answer it.

Even after he'd been told to shut up. Not in so many words, but still...

Shutting up wasn't necessary when there was no one around to hear what you were saying, was it?

That, at least, seemed logical. When there'd been more people on board the *Void*, he'd certainly heard them mutter under their breath specifically so *no one* would hear them, and that hadn't stopped them from talking.

If it was good enough for them, it was good enough for him.

So there.

"What about the *other* threat in the message?" he asked the deserted med-center. "What about the *secret* this Krepnick person said he'd expose?"

Just how important was *that*?

And why didn't Gus want the Captain to know?

CHAPTER 3

Alexander Krepnick.

A name Gus Light had hoped she would never hear again.

A despicable, evil, ruthless man she'd hoped she would never, *ever* hear from again.

AI Bruce had almost spilled the beans on that one. It was hit or miss whether Drake would know the name, but Gus hadn't wanted to take any chances. Drake had never served in the Alliance military. Most civilians went about their lives just fine never knowing a man like Krepnick existed.

Drake wasn't like most civilians. He wasn't like most men period, which was one of the many reasons she loved him. She didn't want to clue him in about Krepnick until she figured out a way to tell Drake something she swore she would never breathe a word of to another living soul.

Not until she figured out whether she even needed to

tell Drake about the most awful, most intentionally terrible thing she'd ever done in her life.

She could feel his eyes on her as she entered the coordinates in Krepnick's transmission into the *Golden Void's* navigation console. They were going to have to open a series of transit flumes to get there. Apparently when the ring ship had winked out of existence, it had relocated to the ass end of known Frontier space to an area that might as well have been a spot on one of the ancient pirate maps from old Earth Drake had collected in his travels. A spot marked *There Be Monsters Here.*

Not exactly a good omen since the last battle they'd been in—a battle they'd won by the skin of their teeth—was against a fleet comprised of half a dozen factions of pirates all after a bounty of singularium, the most sought-after, most *valuable* metal in known space.

Singularium that just happened to form the hull of the self-same massive ring ship Krepnick was sending them to find.

Even thin layers of lightweight singularium were impervious to damage from energy weapons like lasers. Only projectile weapons had a shot at damaging a singularium-plated hull, and then only after the singularium had been bombarded with powerful alternating magnetic forces.

The ring ship was dead in Frontier space when a salvager named Layla Crosscut ran across it. As far as she was concerned, the ship was a derelict and open to salvage claims by the first person who discovered it. Namely her.

All she had to do was defend her claim. Easier said than done.

Crosscut had no idea what the ring ship had been built

for, and she didn't care. All she was interested in was the singularium on its hull. She intended to scavenge all of that precious metal she could. The work would take her years, but it would make her insanely wealthy.

She'd only managed to remove a miniscule percentage of the overall amount of singularium on that huge ship before an all-out battle broke out over competing claims to the ship. Drake and Gus agreed to help Crosscut defend her claim in exchange for some of the singularium.

Then everything went to hell when Jorritz Tor decided *he* wanted the ship. To back up his claim, he put together an army of so many different pirate factions they were nigh on unbeatable.

Gus wasn't about to let Tor win this battle. So she'd called in every favor she could think of, including getting help from an old friend—an independent reporter named Kymmie—to recruit an army to not only defeat Tor, but take him back to the Alliance for a little well-deserved and long-delayed justice.

During the final battle for the ring ship, Gus had learned the ship's real purpose.

It created transit flumes.

Not just any transit flumes, but *massive* transit flumes.

How massive?

Naturally occurring, stable transit flumes could transport varying numbers of ships at a time, depending on the flume's size, but only over relatively short distances. Ships like the *Golden Void* could create artificial transit flumes, but those were just big enough to enable a few ships at a time to travel over even shorter distances. The problem was the amount of power it took to create even a small transit flume. The *Golden Void* had to shut down non-essential systems to create anything more than a puddle-jump sized flume. That was why it was going to take multiple transit flumes to get the *Void* to the ring ship's new location.

The ring ship was built to create transit flumes that could transport an entire *fleet* of ships at one time through a flume that could stretch from the heart of the Alliance to anywhere—*anywhere*—in known space.

Because the ring ship was powered by a contained singularity.

Basically, program in the coordinates to any point in known space, engage the tech, and the ship opened a transit flume that stretched from the center of the ring ship to the spot where you wanted to end up. Any wonder the ship was the most top secret of top-secret projects developed by the Alliance's military intelligence division? With tech like that, the Alliance military could send an entire *fleet* to any point in space in only the time it took to travel through the flume.

It would make the Alliance military unbeatable.

At least, that was the theory.

Early tests with transit flumes that covered only relatively short distances were successful. Unmanned test ships went in the transit flume in the center of the ring ship and came out the other end exactly where they were supposed to.

The military intelligence science dweebs were ecstatic.

Then the tech flamed out in spectacular fashion on the ship's first ultra-long-distance test.

The unmanned test ship went in the transit flume but

never came out at the other end. Worse than that, the ring ship *itself* disappeared into the flume.

Poof! Winked out of existence as if it had never been. And did *not* appear at the coordinates for the other end of the flume.

Scientific heads rolled. Some literally. Covert military intelligence operatives throughout known space were alerted to keep an eye out for any reports of a derelict ship the size and shape of the ring ship.

One of those covert agents, Garrison Brukowski, had served with Gus in the 83rd for a while. When Kymmie contacted Brukowski about joining the fight and he realized the battle was over the missing ring ship, his handler directed Brukowski to not only join the fight, but to render the ring ship's tech inoperative.

Krepnick must have freaked out. As much as a man like Krepnick *could* freak out. The ring ship was not only in the Frontier, it was at the heart of a war waged by Jorritz Tor, the self-described emperor of the Frontier who had designs on invading the Alliance. If Tor won the war and figured out how to make the damn ship work, Tor could transport his entire invasion force into the heart of the Alliance before the military even knew what was happening.

Better to destroy something than have it fall into enemy hands. So Krepnick let Brukowski's instructions stand.

Gus had tried to stop Brukowski from sacrificing himself for the cause. She'd just about convinced him when the damn ship malfunctioned *again,* winking out of existence. Poof redux!

Only this time the ship took Brukowski with it.

No doubt he was dead by now. From what Gus had seen

33

of its insides, the ring ship was never meant to carry a crew. Which made sense. Working close to a contained singularity for any length of time was a death sentence, and Brukowski and the ship had been gone for weeks.

Gus had thought that was the last she'd see or hear about the damn ring ship, and good riddance. All she wanted was to live the rest of her life by Drake's side. Do a few jobs here and there to keep body and soul together. Earn enough to afford a drink of the good stuff every now and then while she listened to Drake strum a few ancient cowboy songs on his antique guitar.

Krepnick had turned up like the proverbial bad penny to skudge the whole thing up.

A man like Krepnick wouldn't care one whit about Brukowski. He didn't care about anybody or anything other than his precious Alliance.

So Krepnick had co-opted Gus and Drake into working for military intelligence.

Somehow, probably through reports Brukowski had sent back to his handler, Krepnick knew about AI Bruce. Knew that Bruce was more than just a standard ship's computer.

The transmission hadn't come right out and said that. That was the problem with military intelligence. With men like Krepnick in particular. They never said *anything* flat out, in plain language, that could be used against them. But Gus could read between the lines.

She'd told Drake that the transmission instructed her to locate the ship and claim it, or what's left of it. What she hadn't told him was they were instructed to claim the ship on behalf of its rightful owner so it could be *returned* to that owner.

The Alliance military science division.

The coordinates Krepnick had given her were deep in the Frontier. The only way to return the ring ship to the Alliance military was to get its transit flume generator operational enough to send the ring ship itself through the flume and back to Alliance space.

Gus was a good mechanic. She'd modified her armor herself so many times that she could do things in her armor no armor jock should be able to do.

But even she couldn't fix whatever was wrong with the ring ship.

AI Bruce, with his Fluke-enhanced abilities, might— *might*—be able to do that.

Failing that, Krepnick wanted the ring ship destroyed, once and for all. And he wanted proof that the ship was destroyed, not just winked out of existence again.

If Gus couldn't make that happen, Krepnick would destroy Kymmie. Hell, he'd probably destroy AI Bruce too, not to mention Drake and the *Golden Void* and anybody else who'd ever seen the ring ship.

Compared to all that, the secret Krepnick threatened to expose seemed like such a small thing.

She took a deep breath and turned away from the nav console. Drake was sitting in the captain's chair, strumming a few chords on his antique guitar. The chords weren't to any particular song. He was just using the music to center himself.

To get himself ready for whatever was coming.

She really needed to give him a heads up. It was only fair.

She walked over to him, lifted the guitar off his lap, and sat down in its place.

"This mean we're ready to go, darlin'?" he asked.

She brushed his hair away from his forehead. He had a few more lines there than when she'd first met him. Not exactly battle scars, more like reminders that life with her wasn't always sweetness and light. She supposed she had more lines on her own forehead, not to mention a couple of mostly healed scars on her shoulder where she'd taken enemy fire that slipped in between the sections of her armor where it was the weakest.

"In a minute," she said, gazing into his eyes.

Had anyone ever trusted her as much as this man? Maybe her son's father, but that had been a lifetime ago. Drake had been betrayed in his past by at least one woman he'd loved that Gus knew of, possibly more. She didn't want to ever make him think that she'd betrayed him too. That meant she'd have to come clean with him.

She leaned forward and gave him a light kiss on the lips.

When they parted, she said, "I need to tell you a story."

To his credit, he didn't say anything. Her laid-back cowboy knew her so well. If it was her story to tell, he'd let her tell it in her own way.

"It happened a long time ago," she said. "And it involved a man named Alexander Krepnick."

CHAPTER 4

Brukowski wasn't dead. He just felt that way sometimes.

Like now.

KZZZZTT!

Strapped into the too-familiar cradle of a device aboard the alien ship that had "rescued" him weeks ago, he threw his head back and screamed his lungs out. Each of the dozens of beams of blazing white light shooting into him felt like a superheated dagger being driven into his body for the sole purpose of inflicting pain.

He knew it was doing much more than that, though. Between screams and tears, he glimpsed images on a huge video screen on the wall of his torture chamber—images pulled from his memory and replayed like a movie of the past. Some of them were scenes of simpler, happier times... pleasant picnics, gorgeous sunsets, warm kisses from pretty women.

But most of them recalled violent times from his military

career—brutal battles, the deaths of comrades, the murders of enemies. For whatever reason, those were the memories on which the aliens focused the most...those, and his recollections of certain vessels that had been part of the fleet assembled by the Gray Lady—Gus Light—to defeat Jorritz Tor's forces in the Battle of the ring ship.

Brukowski had been instructed to join Light's fleet. It should have been the perfect cover for a covert military intelligence agent.

Not that his handlers gave a rip about Jorritz Tor, a disgraced Alliance ambassador with delusions of building an empire in the Frontier strong enough to challenge the Alliance. They hadn't given a rip about Brukowski either, but he'd gone to work for military intelligence with his eyes wide open.

Or so he'd thought. Torture by aliens hadn't been part of the deal.

Two ships in that battle—living spacecraft belonging to a starfaring species known as the Ongoni—had been unlike any vessels he'd seen or traveled on...at least until his current imprisonment.

The smaller of the vessels had been part of Light's fleet. It had the shape of a seagoing manta ray, its body one wide, rippling wing. Light had called it the *Scintilla* and said it responded to the thoughts and wishes of its pilot.

The other, much larger vessel had been claimed by Tor as his personal ship. It resembled a massive bird of prey, like an eagle, complete with a razor-sharp beak and banks of missiles in place of claws. Both ships had hulls of the same glossy black material, a biological matrix like that of the spacecraft in which Brukowski was now held prisoner.

Though he didn't know the name of the current ship, if indeed it even had one, Brukowski had dubbed it the *Hellspawn* for obvious reasons.

KZZZZTT!

The beams of light piercing him from projectors inside the canopy over his cradle suddenly intensified. Brukowski shrieked and thrashed mindlessly as the latest wave of blinding agony sizzled through him.

For what must have been the millionth time, he wished he'd never leaped out of the singularium-clad ring ship. For that matter, he wished he'd never boarded the ring ship in the first place, but he'd been following orders to render it inoperative in the midst of the battle between Light's and Tor's forces. He'd still been trapped inside the damn thing trying to follow those orders when the ship transported itself to a sector of space with absolutely no recognizable star systems.

No nearby planets.

No nearby space stations.

No food. No water. No nothing.

He'd thought that he was a dead man.

Then he'd spotted a ship hovering nearby, and he'd made the worst mistake of his life. He'd handed himself over to the *Hellspawn* in the hope of salvation. If only he'd known he'd be taken captive and subjected to *this*…and that his own memories were being tapped and somehow put to use in ways he couldn't fully understand.

Or maybe he could.

A theory had come to him after all the hours of abuse— and all the hours of isolation without human companionship. It was a theory he didn't like to think about, especially given his possible role in bringing a certain horrific end result to fruition.

Clearly, the aliens who controlled *Hellspawn* were studying his memories...some more than others. They wanted to learn something in particular, perhaps to improve their own mastery of one particular skill.

Killing.

Maybe, he thought, they wanted to get better at *killing.*

But for what reason?

KZZZZTT!

Again, the beams flared brighter, and Brukowski shrieked and bucked. The restraints remained firmer than ever, unaffected by his wild movements.

Around the torture cradle, several bipedal robots stood and watched him with emotionless eyes like ping pong balls with horizontal black slits. Of everything he'd observed aboard the ship, they were the most humanoid, the structure of their bodies roughly corresponding to the human form. Brukowski had a feeling they weren't standard equipment, though—that perhaps they'd been whipped up specifically to handle him after his capture. If so, the least the aliens could have done was given them voices and allowed them to interact with him...but they hadn't. The robots moved him from room to room, connected and disconnected various devices to him, brought him *very* basic liquids and foodstuffs to supplement whatever they were pumping into his belly to keep him alive, and never said a word while doing it.

The aliens never communicated with him, either, which was driving him insane. He'd never even seen them. Didn't know if there was just one alien directing his torture or an entire crew. The *Scintilla* had done whatever its pilot told it to do, including creating tools for the pilot to use. The alien who was creating *Hellspawn's* torture tools was one skudging bastard.

Brukowski had no way of knowing how long he'd been on this ship. The armor he'd worn in space was gone, and with it any way to tell the passage of time. The aliens let him sleep only long enough to keep his body alive before the robots moved him back to this chamber and his torture started all over again.

His beard and hair were growing, he knew that. How long would that take? He didn't know. He'd never let himself grow a beard before. Weeks, maybe. And in all those weeks of captivity, he'd learned nothing of his captors' true intentions...or his own ultimate fate.

In darker moments, he wondered if he'd be kept here for the rest of his life, tortured relentlessly until his body finally gave out. He wondered if he might never see the familiar stars of the Alliance again, if all those people and places he cared about were forever out of reach.

And he wondered about other things, too...like what had happened beyond the hull of the *Hellspawn* during his time inside it. None of the rooms in which he was held had even a tiny porthole view of space outside the ship.

Was the ring ship still nearby, or had it flashed away to even more distant sectors, propelled by its singularity-based transit flume system?

If the ring ship was still here, did the Ongoni have plans for it, and if so, how far forward were they? They were interested in it, that much was clear from what they'd plundered from his memories. Not that he knew much beyond what the ship was supposed to do when it actually worked and how to render it inoperative. He sure as hell didn't know how to fix it.

For that matter, what about Military Intelligence and *their* plans for the ring ship? The ring ship was a top-secret project. Brukowski's orders had come directly from within Military Intelligence, and it was his experience that M.I. didn't like sharing their toys with anyone. As a product of their R&D, it belonged to them, after all, and could prove a potent destabilizing force in the interstellar balance of power. With its ability to instantaneously transport entire fleets of ships via transit flume across vast distances, it was the very definition of a game-changer.

Given that incredible power, wouldn't Military Intelligence do absolutely everything they could to find the ring ship again...and find *him* in the bargain? Was there then some hope of discovery and rescue after all?

Or would the Ongoni and *Hellspawn* be ready to repel *anyone* who tried to come between them and their find? Worse, what if their probing of his long experience as a *killer* made them an even greater force to be reckoned with, one that could not be defeated?

What if Brukowski, who for most of his life had been as patriotic as they came, ended up giving the ultimate enemy the weapons they needed to destroy the very Alliance he had always served and adored?

KZZZZTT!

Again, he wailed for release...but nothing changed. The robots continued to stare silently, and visions from his memories continued to flicker across the huge viewscreen.

He saw scenes from a beach vacation long ago...then

moments from Christmas holidays throughout the years. Then, in brutal counterpoint, he saw himself gunning down enemy soldiers in a desert battle under a blistering sun. He saw a fellow warrior blowing away unarmed villagers in the jungle and a bomb dropping from a giant aircraft to vaporize an enormous city.

Then he saw a massive armored figure, an armor jock spraying hundreds of rounds a second into an approaching enemy army. He saw another armor jock leap in from a great height and change the attack, blasting away the ground in front of the army instead of mowing down the ragtag rank of advancing fighters.

He would recognize that jock anywhere, even without seeing her enter the armor. He knew Gus Light's battlefield style by heart and well remembered the moment captured onscreen as he watched.

From there, he saw a whole procession of memories that featured Gus in action...culminating in her armored exit from the launch bay of that cowboy's ship, the *Golden Void*, to hunt him down on the ring ship. Even with the many years when they'd been away from each other's orbits, he had loads of memories of her...and the *Hellspawn* Ongoni seemed fascinated by those particular memories for some reason.

Suddenly, then, the speed at which the memories displayed accelerated. They flickered over the screen at a breathtaking rate, hypnotically dancing before his watery eyes.

Then they stopped, and the screen went blank. For a long moment, nothing appeared there, and the room was silent.

But the silence didn't last. A loud pinging sound echoed through the room, repeating again and again like the noise of a submarine's sonar.

Ping...ping...ping...ping

Was something or someone being summoned by that signal? If so, to what end?

KZZZZTT!

And would there be anything left of Brukowski by the time they got there?

CHAPTER 5

Thirty-five years ago...

Gus Light hated the last few moments before deployment.

She hated anything that made her wait. Waiting gave her time to think, and thinking was a soldier's worst enemy.

She was an armor jock. Armor jocks weren't supposed to think. They were supposed to follow orders. Do their job, and the job was killing.

That's what she'd signed up for, right? The squadrons of the 83rd Armor Division of the Free Worlds Alliance military were the best of the best. As a raw recruit, she'd fought tooth and nail to be one of them. They were renowned through the Alliance. One-person killing machines, armed to the proverbial teeth, each and every one of them.

Now at twenty-five years old, Augusta "Gray Lady"

Light was already being hailed as the hero of the 83rd for her decisive, *deadly* action on the battlefield. Balls to the wall, people called her style. Balls of steel, her squadron mates said.

"Gray Lady got them balls of *steel*, my man," more than one had said. Sometimes grudgingly, sometimes with pure admiration. "You don't screw with her lest you want your head handed to you."

Did any of them know she'd ripped her own heart and soul out and left them behind with an infant son on a world where she could never set foot again? That she'd left behind her son's father, now dead and buried on that same world?

That she had nothing left inside *except* the job?

Easy to be balls-to-the-wall when you didn't care if you lived or died. Except when you had too much time to think. Then you started caring.

Then you started thinking you should do something about it.

Countdown commence.

The order flashed on the heads-up display inside her armor's visor.

Normally a thirty-second countdown, this time the countdown started at ten.

Less time to think. Gus approved.

Nine... eight... seven...

The bay doors of the transport opened beneath her squadron's feet. Twelve armor jocks held suspended by the clamps on their armors' shoulders, the ground zooming past far below as the transport screamed toward the drop zone.

Six... five... four...

Gus took a deep breath, closed her eyes briefly as she flexed her hands inside her armor's gauntlets. All armament was online. The enhancements she'd made to her armor read green across the board.

She was ready.

Three... two...

Ready to kill.

One!

Clamps released. The squadron, Gus among them, fell toward the surface already in formation. Twelve metal killing machines, armed and ready for battle.

Ready to wage war.

In a fight against children.

Armor jocks were trained to see the enemy not as individuals but as targets on the heads-up display inside their armor's visor.

You couldn't kill people if you thought of them as *people*. They were targets, pure and simple.

Destroy the target. Move on. Destroy the next target. Avoid getting fragged, then move on to the next target.

Rinse and repeat.

And by God, stay in formation.

Gus had trouble with that last part. She always had. That had been the one consistent knock against her during her training. She wouldn't wait for the less competent cadets in her training squadron to catch up with her. That had changed once she found a squadron leader she could respect. They'd butted heads initially, then they'd each grown to respect the other.

Respect had turned to love, and when love had produced an unplanned pregnancy, they'd planned to leave the military to raise their child, reupping after the child was grown.

That hadn't happened.

When her son's father died, so had Gus's respect for every squadron leader who came after him. The worst in her opinion was the squadron's newest leader, a wet-behind-the-ears lieutenant whose name she refused to learn.

This new man only wore the armor because he believed service as an armor jock—as one of the *men,* as he put it—would give him a step up the advancement ladder over men who'd never worn the suit. Who'd never seen action.

The lieutenant took his squadron wherever he was ordered to go, but the battle plans he made, the orders he gave, were always scorched earth. Overkill. Anything to make sure that his own precious metal-encased hide never got so much as a scratch while he led the squadron into battle.

He was a coward, and Gus refused to follow the orders of a coward.

Oh, she always stayed in formation during the drop. Stayed in formation just long enough to assess each situation, then she executed her own battle plans.

There was a reason she was hailed as a hero. She made the 83rd look good. And because she made the 83rd look good, that made the lieutenant look good. He might berate her in private in a vain attempt to make her toe his own brand of the company line, but in public? He was all smiles, taking credit for sending his "secret weapon" into battle as his lone wolf warrior. To confound the enemy, he said, with her unorthodox battle style.

Gus loathed the man.

She never loathed him more than she did now because his battle plans called for annihilating children.

Gus didn't know why the 83rd had been sent into this particular battle. Didn't understand or care to understand the politics behind the decision. She had at one point. Before, when her life had meaning. When her son's father, himself a student of history, had sparked her interest in ancient Earth's political battles and their correlation to Alliance politics and policies.

Then she'd become disillusioned with politics when she'd seen firsthand how easily the unethical could manip-ulate the naïve with no concern for the wreckage left behind in their wake.

The enemy targets, the lieutenant had told his squadron, were guerilla fighters. That's all they needed to know. Their heat signatures had been programmed into each armor jock's heads-up display. Eliminate the targets with laser fire from the armor jocks' shoulder-mounted launchers. They wouldn't even have to get close. The enemy targets didn't possess sophisticated weaponry.

The lieutenant expected his squadron to take no casualties.

That's why he was leading the charge.

Against children.

Gus had made the mistake of zooming in on the leading edge of the enemy formation. It appeared they were attacking with homemade weapons. Spears tipped with sharpened pieces of metal. Freaking bows and *arrows*. Rocks hurled from handheld launchers.

Armor jocks were supposed to take these fighters out with *laser* weapons? The lasers fired from each armor jock's shoulder-mounted launchers were powerful enough to bring down a building. None of the weapons these fighters were using would even cause a dent in her armor much less actually do her any harm.

And when did guerillas resort to using weapons that looked like little more than the toys Gus and her friends had played soldier with when she'd been little?

That's when she switched her armor's heads-up display to show her the faces of the enemy.

That's when she discovered her squadron had been ordered to kill children.

Not disarm them. Not render them ineffective.

Kill them.

She'd lost it then.

She didn't care why they were fighting. She didn't care who they were fighting against or why the Alliance had taken sides against them.

They were freaking *children*. None of them looked older than preteen. She wasn't going to let her squadron kill them.

So she did what she'd always done.

She'd gone rogue. Gone off script.

She'd used all the power in her armor and attacked the ground in front of the enemy.

She'd blasted in from above them, using the specialized maneuvering jets she'd installed on her armor, and dug a trench so wide and so deep that the advancing army of *children* had no hope of crossing it.

The lieutenant was screaming at her over her comm channel. Demanding to know what the *skudge* she thought she was doing.

"I ordered an all-out assault!" he screamed. Then he opened the channel to the entire squadron. "Carry out my orders! You are to eliminate the enemy targets. *Now!*"

To their credit, none of the armor jocks followed his orders. They stopped on the other side of the trench Gus had opened and stood, shoulder-mounted launchers in the ready position.

The enemy targets, the *children*, dropped their weapons.

"You heard me!" the lieutenant screamed. "Shoot!"

So Gus did.

"Krepnick found out about it," Gus told Drake.

She was still sitting on his lap in the pilot's chair of the *Golden Void*. Even thirty-five years later, she could still feel the absolute raw hatred that had coursed through her when she aimed her launcher at her squadron's lieutenant and blasted him into oblivion.

"He wasn't the director of military intelligence then," she said, "but he was on his way up. I don't know how he knew what I did. No one in the squadron breathed a word of what happened. I think they all would have done the same thing, but everyone knew I was the only one who might get away with killing a commanding officer and not be put to death for it."

She looked in Drake's kind, compassionate eyes. It only made her feel worse.

"Back then I was willing to die," she said. "I was *ready* to die to save those kids. Krepnick made it clear to me that was a viable possibility should he ever decide to make my actions go public, and he'd implicate the rest of my squadron for covering up what happened." She took a deep breath. "That's what was in the rest of the message. That's why I don't have a choice. Krepnick's a ruthless man, far worse than anyone we've ever encountered, and I'm including Jorritz Tor. That's what we're really up against. So if you want to bail, I understand. Just say the word. I'll still love you no matter what."

She just hoped that now that he knew she'd deliberately murdered a commanding officer and the director of military freaking intelligence was threatening to use that against her, the laidback cowboy she loved would still love her.

CHAPTER 6

Drake gazed at Gus for a long moment, choosing his words carefully. As rough and tumble as both of them could be, the relationship between them was a fragile thing, not to be taken lightly.

Blundering in like a bull in a balloon animal rodeo after she'd just got done baring her soul could blow it all to pieces.

And that was the *last* thing he wanted to do. After everything they'd been through together and everything they'd come to mean to each other, Augusta Light was the most precious thing in the universe to him. He would do pretty much anything to keep her safe and close, sacrifice whatever it took, including himself.

Scratch that. He wouldn't do *pretty much* anything. He would do *anything*.

"Darlin'." He brushed his fingers over her short gray hair. "Thank you for tellin' me all that."

She nodded once, her eyes locked on his, expectant. Waiting for whatever he said next.

He didn't dare let her down.

"I'm so sorry you went through that," he told her. "That you had to make that choice to save those kids…and save yourself."

That, of course, was the root of it, he knew. If she'd followed the lieutenant's orders, she would have stayed in his good graces; she would have avoided opening herself up to possible blackmail down the line, as was now happening. She could've justified taking that terrible action, telling herself she'd only been following orders.

But she would have lost *herself* in the process. She would have had to live the rest of her life with the knowledge that she'd violated the dictates of her own conscience, that she'd done something awful when she could have prevented it. In the process, she would have become a very *different* Gus Light…perhaps even a Gus Light that Drake might not have fallen in love with.

And robbing him of the joys of loving her would have been a crime he couldn't bear to contemplate.

"Given the circumstances, I have no doubt you did the right thing. You always do." He continued to stroke her hair, then her cheek. They were no longer brand-new to each other, but touching her still electrified him. "It's one of the things I love best about you, darlin'…one of many."

Her eyes glistened, wet with the force of emotion if not the start of tears.

"And that love will never change," he said softly. "And I will never bail out on you. *Never*." Smiling, he felt the full force of his devotion radiate outward, bathing her like rays of intense starlight. "Got that?"

She nodded and leaned in to kiss him. He could feel her own love beaming back at him with a strength at least the equal of his own.

So this was what he'd been missing all his life, without ever quite knowing it until now. The shallow little dalliances over the years may have satisfied him physically, perhaps nudged aside some basic human loneliness now and then...but none of them had ever measured up to the love he felt for Gus. None of them had brought this level of trust and faith and intimacy, such that no secret could threaten the connection between them.

If ever he did somehow lose her, lose this, he knew he would be a broken man. If someone had told him just a few years ago that he—the free-and-easy space cowboy, kicked-back smuggler, happy-go-lucky drifter—would be like that, he never would have believed them.

But now he knew, with all his heart, that it was true.

And he would never give up any of it without the fight to end all fights.

"As for this Krapnick bastard..." His mispronunciation was intentional, for her benefit. "...I say we make him *regret* this little blackmail scheme of his as much as any *skudge-hole* has ever regretted *anything*."

She looked at him for a long moment, no doubt trying to gauge how serious he was. "He's ruthless," she said. "I mean that. He's got his fingers in all sorts of pies."

"Then I say we chop 'em off. Right down to the bone."

Could they do that? Why the hell not?

Now she was starting to grin. "A new version of the Smiley Face Gambit?"

"Call it the Skudge-Hole Takedown," he said. "How's that sound?"

"Like you're speakin' my language, cowboy." Again, she kissed him…only longer and more forcefully this time.

When they both came up for air, Drake held her face in his hands and smiled. "Good to know we're on the same page, Gray Lady."

"It's the only page we ever need," she told him.

"So what do you say?" he asked. "Ready to go find this ring ship again and make Krapnick wish he'd never blackmailed us into takin' the job?"

She nodded. "Funny thing is, I suddenly wanna get to that ship more than *ever*, just so we can take it away from him."

Or turn it against him, Drake thought. Wouldn't that just be a hoot and a half. He'd outwitted the Fluke more than once. Outwitting this bastard wouldn't be easy, but if experience had taught Drake anything, it was that doing something unexpected—even something *stupid*—was the best way to beat someone who thought they were unbeatable. He was damn good at doing unexpected, stupid shit and having it work out.

Drake chuckled. "I like the way you think."

"We oughtta be ready to head out by now." She raised her voice enough to get the AI's attention. "Am I right, Bruce?"

"The course from the encrypted message is laid in, ma'am," Bruce said over the intercom speaker. "Just give the word, and we'll launch."

Gus's brow wrinkled. "Since when have you ever called me 'ma'am,' Bruce?"

"Since now," said Bruce with the vocal equivalent of a shrug. "Would you prefer something less formal, like 'battle-chick' or 'baby' or…"

"Nope!" Gus rolled her eyes. "'Ma'am' is fine for now, thanks."

"Very good, ma'am," said Bruce. "Launching when ready, ma'am."

Gus and Drake both laughed. Bruce's uneven behavior wasn't always well-timed, but the comic relief was welcome at the moment. On the verge of beginning another quest into certain danger with ample unknowns, a chuckle at the AI's expense was a good way of relieving pressure.

Just as a pillow fight was a good way of passing the time between departure and arrival.

Did Drake have the idea first? Somehow, when he gazed into Gus's eyes, he knew she was on the same wavelength.

There was work to be done on the trip to the ring ship's location, but they should still be able to fit in a decent pillow fight…and whatever other pleasurable activities it might lead to.

"Bruce?" Drake patted Gus's back, and she got up from his lap. "Lock in that course and let's ride."

"Will do, pardner," Bruce said in an accent that recalled the old Earth movie cowboy, John Wayne. "Yeehaw!"

Drake caught the twinkle in Gus's eye, and his grin widened. *Yeehaw* indeed.

"Don't spare the horses," he told Bruce on his way to the exit behind Gus. "The sooner we round up that ring ship, the better."

"Roger that, Cap'n," said Bruce. "I'm cooking up a primo transit flume as we speak."

"Love it." Drake followed Gus through the door, then leaned back into the room. "Oh, and Bruce? Bring us in just far enough from the ring ship coordinates that we won't likely get spotted by whoever else might be there."

"Do you expect company, Cap?" asked Bruce. "Those coordinates are in the middle of nowhere."

"Doesn't matter," said Drake. "A ship like that with a singularium hull attracts scavengers like a dead horse in the desert attracts vultures."

Bruce paused. "You think we're heading for a fight, then?" He did not sound unexcited.

"I *always* expect a fight," said Drake. "They have a way of breaking out whenever I show up."

As he said it, Gus grabbed his arm and yanked him out into the hallway, impatiently pulling him in the direction of their quarters, where the pillows awaited.

CHAPTER 7

Military intelligence.

The only way to survive—to *thrive*—long term in military intelligence was to have an ace up your sleeve.

The man known as Agent Zero to a certain pain-in-the-ass reporter named Kymmie had a definite ace up his sleeve. He'd kept that ace hidden for long years, just waiting for the right time to bring that particular card into play. And that damn reporter had ruined everything.

She'd not only recorded evidence of the existence of the ring ship, something no one outside of the Military Intelligence Division even knew existed, she'd been recording when the skudging ship up and disappeared.

Again.

Then she'd threatened to expose that information by providing those recordings to an entire network of Alliance-wide independent news outlets. News outlets that were so independent they purposefully thumbed their collective noses at any attempt to control the content of their reports.

Agent Zero should know. In his position as an Assistant Director of Military Intelligence in charge of a wide swath of Alliance space bordering the Frontier, he had attempted to exert gentle influence on those outlets in the past. Just to see how far they would bend.

The answer had been: not at all.

Kymmie had put him in a bind. He couldn't just disappear her. She'd ingratiated herself with too many people, including former military armor jocks who were both notoriously loyal and notoriously difficult to control. Including the damn Gray Lady herself, Augusta Light, the most difficult soldier who'd ever served in the Alliance's Armor Division. They'd make a stink about her disappearance. They might even take it upon themselves to figure out what happened to her.

Things like that had a way of getting out of hand. All it would take would be one whistleblower that other reporters—that *politicians*—would listen to. Reporters would file stories, but politicians would convene commissions. Hold public hearings. Might even subpoena him to testify at those hearings.

That would be the death of his career.

Besides, all she'd wanted was a deal. Agent Zero made deals all the time on behalf of military intelligence to keep the military's secrets *secret*. It was practically an unwritten part of his job description.

What Kymmie said she wanted was an exclusive to cover the trial of Jorritz Tor.

The trial of disgraced former Alliance ambassador and

self-proclaimed emperor of the Frontier Jorritz Tor for treason against the Alliance would be the trial of the century. Having an exclusive to not only the courtroom proceedings but all the behind-the-scenes drama would make Kymmie's career. Agent Zero understood her motivation. She was almost as ambitious as he was.

Almost.

So he'd made the deal.

Then she'd said she wanted something else or the deal was off. She wanted the Alliance to clear Gus Light's record.

That had been a harder pill to swallow.

Gus Light had broken so many Alliance laws over the course of her lifetime that Agent Zero had lost count. She'd been a rogue armor jock, ignoring orders whenever she deemed it necessary. She would have been drummed out of the Armor Division if her antics hadn't been so successful. As far as the general public was concerned, she was a hero. More than one of her superiors had ridden her heroics to greater careers within the military.

Light had never sought advancement for herself. In fact, she'd "retired" earlier than most armor jocks when she'd decided to steal her armor rather than see it decommissioned as obsolete.

Agent Zero would have prosecuted her then, hero or no hero.

Except word had come down from Director Krepnick himself that Augusta Light was to be left alone. No prosecution for theft of military property. She was out of their hair, Krepnick said. Since she seemed determined to drink her way through her retirement on an out-of-the-way space station, the military was content to let the Gray Lady and all her past heroics fade into obscurity.

Agent Zero knew what that meant. Krepnick had something in mind for her. Some secret he held over her head. Try as he might, Zero had never been able to figure out what that was. There were blank spots in Light's official record. Places where data had been irretrievably erased. Something had happened in those blank spots that Krepnick didn't want anyone else to find out. He was not only the master of keeping secrets, he was the master of knowing when—and how—to use them.

But even Krepnick couldn't protect Light when she used her stolen military property—her decommissioned armor— to interfere in a civil war on a planet the Alliance had declared off limits. Yet once again Light only got a slap on the wrist. A *don't do it again* and the Alliance would leave her alone. Provided she never reentered Alliance space.

Gus Light was in permanent exile, but she would remain a free woman as long as she remained in the Frontier.

Kymmie wanted all that to go away.

Otherwise she'd tell the world all about the existence of the ring ship *and* the fact that the military had—once again —lost the damn thing.

She hadn't known that the military itself didn't know about the ring ship. That it had been a project developed solely under the military intelligence division.

That it was Director Krepnick's pet project.

So Agent Zero decided to pull some strings to see how far he could get.

It turned out the strings had only needed a slight tug. The reports Kymmie had already filed with her news outlets made it clear that Gus Light had been a hero once again. That even though she was retired, the Gray Lady's allegiance to the Alliance was so strong that she'd risked her own life to almost single-handedly stop an invading force from waging war against the Alliance. How would it look if the Alliance didn't reward Light for her selfless heroics? The military's legal division was downright eager to expunge all outstanding charges against her.

Agent Zero's mistake had been in not involving Director Krepnick in the deal.

Not that Zero knew it was a mistake at the time. Krepnick had always made it clear no charges were to be brought against Light. Ever. Making a deal to negate her exile was just a continuation of that policy.

When Krepnick had summoned Agent Zero to his office, Zero was confident he would be getting a promotion for his efforts.

But Krepnick hadn't been pleased.

He hadn't yelled. He hadn't threatened. He hadn't even demoted Agent Zero.

Not in so many words.

But he had known about an ace Agent Zero had up his sleeve.

An ace no one—absolutely *no one*—should have known about.

Agent Zero had a way to track Gary Brukowski, the covert asset who'd been aboard the ring ship when it disappeared. The same chip embedded in Brukowski's wrist, the chip that allowed Brukowski to send encrypted messages directly to Agent Zero, included a tracking beacon that even Brukowski didn't know about.

The beacon was incredibly powerful. It didn't rely on being surrounded by living tissue to operate. That meant it would continue to transmit its location long after Brukowski was dead, and Brukowski had to be dead by now.

Thanks to that tracking beacon, Zero knew the exact sector of Frontier space where Brukowski had reappeared. Brukowski had been on the ring ship. It stood to reason that where Brukowski ended up was also where the ring ship was.

And Agent Zero thought he was the only one who knew where that was.

He thought he would be able to parlay that information into the position he wanted: Chief Deputy Director of the entire Military Intelligence Division, second only in power to Krepnick himself.

Instead Krepnick had used that information against Agent Zero.

Had told Agent Zero, after a debriefing that had gone from bad to worse to nightmare level over the course of three excruciating hours, that if he wanted to salvage what was left of his career, he would take a ship and go out there, on his own, and blow the damn ring ship up, once and for all.

"Then we'll talk about advancement within the division," Krepnick had said. "If you survive."

If he survived.

That wasn't a given.

The ring ship had ended up in a sector of the Frontier that bordered on Ongoni space. The Ongoni didn't suffer outworlders. As unpredictable and omniscient as the Fluke were, the Ongoni were vicious. No one ever dealt with the Ongoni directly. They built magnificent, highly advanced ships that they rarely sold to outworlders. Even when they did, all contacts were handled through robotic intermediaries.

All attempts to embed operatives in Frontier organizations—legal or otherwise—who were rumored to have dealt with the Ongoni had failed, sometimes spectacularly.

If the Ongoni got their hands, if they even had hands, on the ring ship and got its top-secret transit flume technology to work, they could pose a far deadlier threat to the Alliance than Jorritz Tor and his fleet of pirate invaders. That was the official reason Krepnick wanted the ring ship destroyed.

The unofficial reason?

Krepnick didn't want any evidence that the ring ship had ever existed.

It didn't take a genius to figure out why Krepnick had kept the ring ship and its transit flume technology within the military intelligence division. Krepnick controlled the intelligence division with an iron fist. No one crossed him. Ever. Because Krepnick had a vision for what the Alliance should be, and it wasn't a democracy ruled by politicians from all the disparate worlds within the Alliance. Politicians who only cared about the interests of their own home worlds.

Politicians who refused to work together for the greater good.

Zero wanted to take evidence of the ring ship's existence

back to the Alliance and serve it up on a silver platter to those same politicians as evidence of Krepnick's betrayal of the very Alliance he'd sworn to protect. Krepnick had kept the ring ship's existence secret for so long that the implications would be clear even to empty-headed, self-serving politicians. Whoever controlled the ring ship had the power to control the Alliance itself.

They would see Krepnick's actions as the start of a coup by military intelligence against the Alliance's ruling body. They would force Krepnick out of office. They might even prosecute him.

That would leave the Military Intelligence Division without a director. Who better to appoint to that position than the man who'd brought them incontrovertible evidence of the former director's betrayal? Possibly the *only* evidence if Krepnick disappeared everything and everyone else connected with the project.

As Agent Zero sat in the pilot's chair of the spaceship he'd commandeered for the trip into the far reaches of Frontier space, he consoled himself with visions of Krepnick, disgraced and removed from office. Of himself gazing out over the capitol city from the director's office as Krepnick had done. Of himself using all the covert technology he was certain Krepnick had installed in the director's office while Krepnick grew old and embittered.

Or perhaps Agent Zero wouldn't allow Krepnick to grow old. A man could know too many secrets to be allowed to live. Agent Zero wouldn't be as lenient with Krepnick as Krepnick had been with Augusta Light. After all, Krepnick had sent Agent Zero out here to die.

Agent Zero would have no problems at all returning the favor.

He just had to disappear the ring ship first.

Lucky for him, he knew exactly how to do that.

CHAPTER 8

Travel through transit flumes sped things up, but when you were headed to the ass end of Frontier space, the trip through flume after flume still took a good deal of time.

Time that Gus and Drake put to spectacularly good use.

Maybe it was telling Drake her deepest, darkest secret that did it. The secret that had fueled more than one drunken romp between the sheets simply to let off steam back when her own life hadn't mattered all that much to her. Or maybe it had been Drake's quiet, simple acceptance of what she told him. Not a smidgen of disgust or revulsion or distrust. No pity, either. Somehow that would have been the worst of all.

Or maybe it was the way he'd opened his own soul to her without hesitation.

He'd been hurt before. Hell, he'd been married before, and he'd lost a son of his own. He'd told her about that the night they'd left Shepard's Moon together. Of all the men she'd ever known, Drake would understand why she couldn't follow orders to kill children.

That night on Shepard's Moon had been the true start of them trusting each other on a level she'd begun to think just wasn't possible for someone like her.

A soldier who'd killed on command and drank herself into oblivion to forget about it.

Those days were over now. Truly over.

And as if to prove it, this time after the pillow fight preliminaries were over and they came together beneath Drake's down comforter, Gus lost herself in a whole new way. If she'd opened her eyes to find that her body had melted into his, skin fused together the way she felt their souls were, she wouldn't have been surprised.

He fell asleep afterwards, of course. This time she let him. She was more than content just to snuggle next to him, hear him breathe in and out, and smell the faint scent of cinnamon from the gum he chewed whenever he was about to get down to some serious ass-kicking.

Her laid-back cowboy would have made a hell of a fighter.

Would have?

He *was* a hell of a fighter. A top-notch pilot. As inventive in battle as he was in bed. She couldn't ask for a better person to watch her six.

And they might be in for a fight this time. Drake was right. No matter where the ring ship ended up, there were bound to be scavengers who'd want a piece of it. By the time the *Golden Void* got there, they might be facing who knows what kind of resistance.

That bothered her.

The first time they came across the ring ship, it was because they'd gone looking for the only scavenger anyone knew of who'd managed to run across sufficient supplies of singularium that she was willing to sell some. Singularium was the stuff warriors of all stripes salivated over. Governments too. The fact that singularium had been discovered on Shepard's Moon was the only reason the Alliance had decided to lift its ban on official travel to the planet and reopen negotiations for Shepard's Moon to become an official member of the Alliance.

Gus's armor now had singularium plating on almost every exposed surface. Ditto a large part of the *Golden Void's* hull. It didn't make either Gus or the *Void* invulnerable, but it certainly helped.

The ring ship's entire outer *hull* was covered in singularium.

Except the parts that Crosscut had already removed. Even though she'd relieved the ship of more singularium that her own salvage vessels could hold, that made a nearly infinitesimal dent in the overall amount of singularium on the ring ship's surface.

Claiming a ship like that would make anyone wealthy beyond their wildest dreams.

It would make anyone fight to the death to claim that ship just for the vast amount of singularium alone.

And that wasn't even taking into consideration what the ship could do. *If* the technology was working right. Which apparently it had at one time but now wasn't?

Gus wished she knew more about the ring ship. Wished she'd had time to study its guts when she'd been inside the thing chasing after Brukowski. She was a more than decent engineer, but there hadn't been time to figure out how any of it worked.

There might not be time now, depending on what they found.

She ran a finger down Drake's broad chest.

He didn't even twitch.

One corner of her mouth quirked up in a grin. Give the man a break, she told herself. You wore him out.

She wasn't worn out. Her mind was working overtime, and that was the problem.

She got up and slipped on a pair of casual pants and one of Drake's old-fashioned flannel shirts. The shirt was too big on her, but it smelled like him and she liked that.

She padded out of his cabin on bare feet, the door closing silently behind her. She'd futzed with all the doors on the *Void* during their very first trip to make sure that all of them—except the door to *her* cabin—opened without the normal soft chime. She'd done it just to screw with Drake, but now it let her leave his cabin without disturbing him.

She didn't go to her cabin. The empty bed would have felt too lonely. Truth be told, she never spent much time there anymore, so she should probably stop calling it *her* cabin. He'd started calling his own cabin *their* cabin. Like they'd moved in together or something.

The thought made her grin. She'd never lived with anyone like that. She'd gone from military housing directly to a solitary efficiency apartment that was little more than a place to sleep and shower. The apartment she'd had on Depak Station was even smaller. Two people couldn't have fit inside at once. But with Drake it felt right to share space.

To share pretty much everything.

The corridor outside Drake's—*their*—cabin was dim, the lighting turned down to conserve power, the metal beneath her feet cold. AI Bruce had plotted out the naturally occurring transit flumes they could use to cut down on the amount of flumes the *Void* would need to generate. They must be in a *Void*-generated flume now.

Instead of going all the way up to the bridge, she padded to a nearby auxiliary control room. In an emergency, say if the main bridge was damaged in battle, all essential systems could be controlled from what looked like just another cargo area. There were access panels built into the walls that on first glance looked like just another part of the wall. The panels not only concealed the same kind of old-fashioned controls Drake had installed on the bridge, right down to a steering wheel and joystick, but also concealed access to the crawlspaces that ran the length of the ship.

Before she'd met him, Drake had been a smuggler. The *Void* had a bunch of these hidden panels and compartments, as any halfway decent smuggler's ship should. Gus had explored most of them during her time on the ship.

She wasn't after anything stored in one of the hidden compartments. She wasn't even after the terminals that would show the ship's progress through the various transit flumes.

She wanted to talk to AI Bruce, and she didn't want to disturb Drake while she did it.

The ship's AI was Fluke-enhanced. That didn't mean it necessarily had all the information the Fluke had about the universe. It did have a personality, and that personality was endlessly curious.

That personality had also developed a serious crush on the *Scintilla,* one of the two sentient Ongoni ships that Gus had bought with most of her money after they won the battle with Jorritz Tor. When Gus and Drake decided to take some time for a honeymoon, they'd basically given AI Bruce the keys to the *Golden Void* and let him set the ship's course wherever his Fluke-enhanced personality wanted to go.

Where he'd wanted to go was wherever the *Scintilla* and the second Ongoni ship went.

Ships that Gus was pretty sure were related to each other.

She didn't pretend to understand how the relationships between the two ships worked. She didn't even fully understand how the Ongoni ships communicated with their crew. Drake had said the *Scintilla's* unique abilities were due to something called psiflux engineering, a kind of adaptive shifting tech that changed form and properties at a subatomic level in response to telepathically transmitted thought engrams.

In other words, the *Scintilla's* pilot told the ship what to do with the pilot's mind, and the ship did it.

Gus thought that was a lot of technobabble in an attempt to explain the unexplainable. The larger of the two Ongoni ships had formed a telepathic bond with Gus, going so far as to help Gus capture Tor. Through that bond, the larger Ongoni ship had sent Gus images of her own infant son followed by images of the *Scintilla.* Did that mean the larger ship considered the *Scintilla* its offspring?

That's how Gus had interpreted those images, but who knew if she'd been right about that.

What she was hoping now was for AI Bruce to ask the *Scintilla* what it knew about the ass-end of the Frontier where they were headed.

"Hey, Bruce," she said to the ship's speaker embedded in the wall over one of the access panels. "Feel like having a chat?"

"Always, ma'am!"

Bruce sounded cheerful. And why not? From his perspective, they were on their way to another adventure. So far all their adventures had turned out just fine. He'd never really experienced failure, and Gus hoped they'd be able to keep it that way.

"I'm ready to talk about whatever subject you'd like to discuss," Bruce said. "I've been reviewing ancient Earth mythological texts as they relate to primitive adventure entertainments concerning humans with enhanced abilities. Did you know that certain segments of society believed that exposure to radiation could not only turn a human green or sometimes red, but vastly increase their size while augmenting certain negative emotions?"

Gus blinked. She believed Bruce was referring to something her son's father used to call superhero movies.

"How about we talk about something a little more relevant to our current situation," she said. "Like the area of space we're headed to. You have any insight on that?"

Bruce paused only a moment. "The only references I've been able to locate in Alliance records indicate that area of space borders on territory claimed by the Ongoni, although that area of space itself has not been adequately mapped. Those references appear to be heavily redacted."

Skudge.

Redactions meant military intelligence had covered something up. Probably the existence of covert missions they didn't want anybody to know about. That meant Krepnick had more information about where they were going than Gus did. Or Bruce, for that matter.

But if it bordered on Ongoni territory, maybe the *Scintilla* would know more about it.

"Feel like asking our travel companion about where we're headed?" Gus said.

"Ma'am?"

"The *Scintilla*," Gus said, stopping herself just in time before she added *your girlfriend*.

Both the *Scintilla* and the bigger bird-like Ongoni ship had seemed content to fly along with the *Golden Void* wherever Bruce went. Gus had gotten used to the three ships flying in loose formation for the past couple of weeks.

This time Bruce's pause was a lot longer. While she waited, she lifted a part of Drake's shirt to her face, inhaling his scent and pressing the soft, well-worn fabric against her skin. She'd never been one to run from a fight, but she wouldn't mind putting this one off a little longer.

A sudden shudder ran through the entire ship. The lights in auxiliary control winked off, leaving Gus in the dark.

"Bruce?" she called. "What the hell just happened?"

Had they been attacked?

Bruce didn't answer. Had he gone offline too?

"AI Bruce, respond!"

The lights came back on, only this time the lights in auxiliary control were as dim as they'd been in the corridor.

"Sorry, ma'am," Bruce said. "The transit flume was

breached. It will take a moment to re-establish a stable flume."

Breached?

"How?" Gus asked.

"The *Scintilla* and her companion refused to accompany us any further. They left, rather abruptly."

Gus had never known that a ship could exit a transit flume before traversing its entire length. Especially not an artificially generated flume. Just breaching that much energy distortion, not to mention the rest of the physics involved in creating the flume in the first place... the damn Ongoni ships could have blown the *Void* apart!

"Why the hell did they do that?" she asked.

Bruce sighed audibly. "Once I told them our final destination, they said they were afraid to go anywhere near that sector of space. It seems that the Alliance's knowledge of the Ongoni has been deliberately manipulated by the Ongoni themselves. The *Scintilla* isn't a ship the way the *Golden Void* is a ship. The *Scintilla* and her mother *are* Ongoni. Peaceful Ongoni who lived their lives as free beings in space. Until they were captured by the Dark Dragons."

Gus's anger at their abrupt departure turned to shame.

They'd been so wrong about the *Scintilla* and the bird-like ship. They'd thought that's all they were, just highly advanced ships. And why was that? Just because they looked and acted like ships? Only they were sentient beings, both of them.

And Gus had *bought* them.

Yes, she'd released them, but she'd had to buy them first.

She'd bought another living being. *Two* living beings.

She told herself to focus. She could deal with her feelings later. Bruce had said the *Scintilla* was afraid of being recaptured if they went where the *Void* was headed.

Was the *Void* going to be in danger of being captured too?

"What or who exactly are the Dark Dragons?" Gus asked. "Did the *Scintilla* tell you?"

When Bruce answered this time, his voice held the kind of sorrow that no AI should ever feel. Even an AI with a Fluke-enhanced personality.

"Slavers," Bruce said. "The Dark Dragons are Ongoni slavers, and we're headed directly into their territory."

CHAPTER 9

"Looks like Krapnick's intel was on the money," said Drake. "The giant doughnut's almost exactly where he said it would be."

The image on the main viewer was indeed that of the massive, elusive ring ship, its silver singularium hull gleaming in the reflected light of a nearby star. It was seen from far away, picked up by long-range sensors and magnified by Bruce.

Drake had insisted on staying well back from the ring ship's supposed coordinates, choosing to drop out of a transit flume some distance away. Better to lose a little time approaching the vessel and stay off any scavengers' radar as long as possible.

He was extra glad he'd chosen that strategy as he stared at the image on the viewer. As always seemed to be the case, the ring ship was a magnet for treasure seekers; two vessels, their hulls as black and glossy as those of the *Scin-*

tilla and the bird-shaped craft, were visible in parking orbits alongside the "giant doughnut."

"I see we have company, Bruce." Drake eased himself out of the command chair and stepped forward for a better look at the screen. "Two ships...both Ongoni?"

"Three," corrected Bruce. "One's on the opposite side of the ring ship from us, out of range of our video feed. And yes, sensor data indicates they're all Ongoni."

"Are they Dark Dragons?" asked Gus, who was seated at the navigation console.

"Based on their proximity to Ongoni slaver space, I would say yes," said Bruce, "though I cannot definitively confirm that as yet."

Drake squinted at the two ships visible on the viewer. "Maximum magnification, Bruce."

The image on the screen grew the tiniest bit larger.

"That's max mag now, Captain," said Bruce.

The change was barely noticeable. "Still pretty small," said Gus, "but they look a little like dragons to me."

Drake nodded. The outlines of the Ongoni vessels looked vaguely dragonlike, with broad wingspans, long necks, and bulbous heads...but eyeballing them was insufficient. Until the *Void* got closer and identified them otherwise, he would have to consider them the same hostiles whose mere proximity had been enough to scare away the *Scintilla* and bird ship.

But getting closer presented its own set of problems, of course. If those ships' capabilities were anything like the *Scintilla*'s and bird ship's, they might very well overwhelm the *Void* in close-proximity combat.

And *that* assumed Bruce would even let the *Void*

approach those notorious slavers instead of turning tail to avoid damage and capture. Drake liked to think that battle-tested Bruce wasn't so cowardly, but he wasn't entirely sure the AI wouldn't have second thoughts after his precious *Scintilla* fled the transit flume highway en route to here.

Better, he thought, to expect the best from Bruce and behave as if no possible negative outcome awaited them at the ring ship...none, at least, that was insurmountable.

"We need to go in quiet as we can," said Drake. "Keep a low, low profile."

"Until we blow the living hell out of those slaver bastards," Gus said in her Gray Lady, take-no-prisoners tone of voice.

Drake put his hands on his hips. The ships were too far away to get a decent look at any activity going on near the ring ship.

"Whatever they're doing with the ring ship, it can't be good," he said.

"Trying to take it over, no doubt," said Gus. "Not to mention, they're in our way. We don't get to that ship before they're done doing whatever they're doing, there goes our chance at saving Kymmie."

Drake rubbed his chin and frowned, considering the problem. Even going in slow, with all systems generating as little "noise" as possible—minimizing all forms of energy emissions—the *Void* was bound to attract the Ongonis' attention before long. Once they came after the *Void*, it would be a three-against-one situation; even with her singularium plating and shield generator to repel aggression, the *Void* might not be facing great odds in the coming fight.

If only she had some other means of concealment. Something that even an Ongoni slaver ship with highly integrated, techno-organic systems might overlook.

"I wish we had some kind of cloaking system," he said out loud. "Something to render us undetectable until it's too late for the slavers."

"Actually, Captain," said Bruce, "I might just have a little something up my sleeve that could come in handy."

Drake and Gus shared almost mirror image raised-eyebrow expressions.

What had the AI been up to? Granted, Drake had been spending a whole lot of alone time with Gus. That left the AI free to contemplate whatever a Fluke-enhanced AI thought about when it was alone.

Ancient Earth rock music. Quantum mechanics. The various uses a sheet of singularium could be put to.

But an entire cloaking system?

"You've developed a cloak?" Gus asked, echoing Drake's thoughts.

"Not exactly," said Bruce. "More like the *opposite*, if that makes sense."

Drake liked where this was headed. Bruce taking the initiative didn't always work out exactly right, but the AI had a knack for coming up with outside-the-box insights that could be helpful.

"Tell us more, Bruce," said Drake.

"I was inspired by aspects of my Fluke integration," said Bruce. "In a way, what I've come up with operates the same way the Fluke do—undermining clarity via randomized outputs."

"What kind of outputs?" asked Drake.

"The same ones the *Void* puts out during regular operation," continued Bruce. "Only lots more of them and more scattered. Less predictable...*much* less."

"How do you plan to scatter emissions like that?" said Drake. "If they come from one source—this ship—how will that deceive Ongoni sensors?"

"Because they *won't* come from this ship," said Bruce. "They'll come from mini-drones equipped with energy projectors and scattered across the detection field."

"Hmm." Drake poked at the scheme from every direction he could think of, but it wouldn't fall apart. If Bruce could pull it together as promised, the plan might just make a difference. "You could be onto something there, Bruce."

"Thank you, Captain." Bruce sounded proud of himself. "That means a lot, coming from you."

"I don't hate the idea," said Gus. "And you could modulate the emissions further once we engage the slavers in battle."

"Crank up the output once we start bangin' on 'em." Drake smiled grimly. "Should make a hell of a distraction."

"And of course our own sensors and coms will stay clear as a bell." Gus nodded. "I say we give it a try."

"When can you be ready, Bruce?" asked Drake.

"Five minutes, Captain," Bruce said briskly. "Just need to scan the sensor frequencies the Ongoni are currently using, then tweak the template to compensate."

Drake blinked. Five minutes? It would take the ship's replicator more time than that just to spit out enough mini-drones for the job.

"What about the mini-drones?" Gus asked, once again

echoing Drake's train of thought. "We're talking about a lot of the things to pull this off right."

Drake got it. "Bruce already made them," he said.

"Of course," Bruce said, a hint of affront in his response. "I wouldn't have suggested this course of action if I wasn't prepared to implement it."

Well, that explained some of what Bruce had been doing while Drake and Gus were spending quality time on their not-honeymoon honeymoon. The AI had created a new hobby for itself. Cranking up the ship's replicator to make mini-drones. Good thing the *Void* was well-supplied with raw materials.

Drake rubbed his hands together. "Okay, then. Let me know when you're good to go," he said. "The sooner we get this done, the sooner we stop those slavers from doing whatever they're planning to do with the ring ship."

"Which I can tell you isn't anything good," said Bruce. "According to *Scintilla* before she took off, the slavers have always wanted to expand their operations in a big way. They're obsessed with conquering regions populated by benevolent Ongoni and enslaving their inhabitants. It isn't hard to guess what they might do with the ring ship if they get it up and running."

"That ship could give them what they need for one hell of an expansion," said Gus. "We've seen it open up massive transit flumes to bring an entire fleet from a remote location. The slavers could do the same with a fleet of their own, or worse, duplicate the technology and drop *multiple* fleets deep behind enemy lines."

"Why do you think *Scintilla* and the bird ship left?" asked Bruce. "They went to warn their people of a potential *invasion*…one that could mean the domination of *all* Ongoni in the galaxy by the slavers…the end of free will and freedom of movement for an entire sentient species."

Drake let out a long, low whistle. The scenario was at least as terrible as whatever he and Gus imagined Krapnick had planned for the ring ship technology. The stakes in the game they were playing had just gotten astronomically higher.

"No matter what it takes, we won't let that happen," he said. "Any more than we're gonna let Krapnick turn that ship into a weapon for *his* maniac fantasies…or let Kymmie go down in flames because of him. We've *got* this, yeah?"

Gus smirked. "Hell, yeah."

"Hell yeah, Captain…ma'am," said Bruce.

Rising from the command chair, Drake slid a stick of cinnamon gum from his shirt pocket, peeling the aluminum foil wrapper from around it. "Then I'd say it's time to saddle up, people. Bruce, you get that Fluke Confuser tweaked and ready."

"Will do, Captain, sir!"

"What about you, darlin'?"

Gus's jaw was set as she got up from the nav station. "I'd say it's about time I suited up, Space Cowboy."

"You do that." Taking her face in his hands, he kissed her. "Wouldn't want you to miss out on the fun, Gray Lady."

She kissed him back. "I never do, when I'm with you."

Then she broke away and headed for the door, leaving him to watch her go. As always when she marched off into battle, he felt a pang deep in his belly…a twist of fear as he wondered if he would ever see her alive again. Ever *hold* her again.

But the confident, loving look she shot over her shoulder as she left put that fear to rest. The Gray Lady was in her element on the battlefield and had never known lasting defeat. She *would* return. They *would* reunite. The honeymoon wasn't over until he said it was over.

And *that*, as much as anything, gave him the motivation to fight for all he was worth.

"Bruce!" He folded the stick of gum into his mouth as he always did when the action heated up. "You love to multi-task, don't you?"

"'Love' might be a strong word for it..." said Bruce.

"Like hell it is." Drake grinned and chewed the gum. "Now run a full weapons check while you're getting that Confuser up and running. Make sure those latest upgrades are all spun up and ready for action."

"Yes, sir!"

"I want everything hittin' on all cylinders." Drake grabbed his guitar from the corner, then sat and strummed it in the command chair. "There's some slavers in need of a good ass kickin', and I don't see anyone else around to do it."

CHAPTER 10

The main hold on the *Void* was positively stuffed to the gills with mini-drones.

And that wasn't all.

"Holy crap," Gus muttered under her breath as she made her way around the now-cluttered hold to get to where her armor was stashed.

Bruce had indeed been busy. In addition to what looked like a couple hundred mini-drones, the normally cavernous hold was now home to a super-sized chess board complete with pieces the size of Drake's guitar. The pieces were all sculpted to look like various alien species. At least, Gus thought so. She didn't recognize any of the aliens, and she'd been to a lot of worlds in known space during her time with the 83rd. She guessed the shapes came from conversations Bruce had had with the *Scintilla*. No doubt the *Scintilla* and the bird-like ship had traveled through sectors of space the

Alliance and even the denizens of the Frontier didn't know existed.

At first Gus thought Bruce had used mini-drones to move the pieces around the chessboard.

Then she saw the robot.

It wasn't exactly humanoid. Exactly. It had a torso and two upper appendages that ended in "hands" that had a dozen articulating "fingers" each the size of her own fore-finger. Instead of two legs, it had six long, snake-like cables, each with their own articulating fingers.

The robot was taller than Gus, not that that was hard, but if it stood straight up on those cable-legs, it would be as tall if not taller than her armor. And its head looked *exactly* like her armor's helmet.

"Ah, Bruce?" Gus asked. "Want to tell me what's going on here?"

It took a moment for the AI to answer. When he did, he sounded distracted.

"I was teaching the *Scintilla* to play chess," Bruce said. "She was a very quick study. She created the chessboard you see here inside herself to visualize each move. She suggested I create one here as well."

Of course. The *Scintilla* as well as the bird-like ship could use their bodies to create whatever shapes inside themselves they wanted. That's why everyone thought they *were* ships, just ships that were so highly advanced no human engineer quite understood how they worked, even though they gave it a scientific sounding name: psiflux engineering.

When the Ongoni allowed beings inside themselves,

they shaped their bodies to provide anything their "pilots" thought of. Like a wall, a door, a control console, and even a viewscreen. They even provided breathable atmospheres to emulate the interior of a spaceship.

Bruce had formed a connection with the *Scintilla*. The Ongoni was the AI's version of a first love. And like any besotted teenager, the AI wanted to not only do everything with his new girlfriend, he wanted to *be* with her. Short of transferring his consciousness into the *Scintilla*, the only way Bruce could do that was to replicate the things the *Scintilla* did.

It was like couples Gus had seen who wore the same clothes, ate the same foods, or got matching tattoos. Only in this case, Bruce had done the best he could to create a matching chessboard. He'd reshaped some of the *Golden Void's* supplies into an exact match for the *Scintilla's* chess set. He'd just had to use the replicator to do it. And he'd created the robot to move the pieces on the board.

Around Gus, the mini-drones' ready lights blinked on.

Bruce must have started uploading the new template with the Ongonis' sensor frequencies to the mini-drones. It was almost go time.

Gus started a last-minute check of her armor's systems.

"Should I return the chess set to its component elements?" Bruce asked. "We might need them in the upcoming battle if we need to replicate more mini-drones."

Should he?

Gus had taken nothing with her to remind her of her infant son when she'd been forced to leave him behind. Not a baby blanket or a bootie or even a saved image of him.

89

The only thing she had to remind herself that he even existed was the pain of his birth, and even that faded faster than she would have wanted.

She couldn't ask Bruce to get rid of something that so obviously reminded him of the *Scintilla*. Besides, if things went well, they might run into the *Scintilla* again and Bruce could resume their game.

"Hang onto it for now," she said. "The robot too."

Because who knew when something like that might come in handy?

The mini-drones took to the air, their propulsion systems nearly silent in the cargo hold. These drones were created for space flight, unlike the drones Gus and Drake had fought on Chrysallix that were powered by bladed propellers that sounded like a swarm of angry bees when they lifted off. These drones all had silvery reflective surfaces thanks to a coating of singularium. Gus didn't know where their projectors were hidden and she didn't much care as long as the things worked.

Besides, if Bruce could construct an oversized chess set and uniquely styled robot to run it from just the stuff laying around the *Void*, Gus would trust him to create mini-drones to do what he said they'd do. No wonder Krepnick wanted Bruce along for the ride. If any AI could figure out how to make the ring ship work, it would be the *Void's* Fluke-enhanced Bruce.

Speaking of...

"One last thing, Bruce," Gus said. "Did you put a copy of yourself inside that robot?"

Because something had to be running the robot. Some type of programming, or at the very least some type of input module for the robot to receive instructions on what chess pieces to move and where.

Again, it took Bruce a moment to respond as the first phalanx of mini-drones headed toward the airlock. Drake probably had Bruce running checks on the *Void's* weapons systems. The poor AI was multi-tasking its little Fluke-enhanced brains out.

"It has a portion of my programming installed," Bruce answered.

"So not as advanced as the Little Bruces?"

Bruce had replicated his programming, right down to his enhanced personality, and installed those copies in each of the ships in the ragtag army Gus and Drake had put together to fight Jorritz Tor. For ease of identification, they'd called the copies Little Bruces. The ships had been leased by Exchequer thanks to Drake's annoying sister Persephone, an Exchequer representative. To keep Exchequer aka Persephone happy after the battle was over, they'd left the copies of the Little Bruces installed on the ships.

Every now and then Gus hoped they hadn't unleashed a new plague of Fluke-enhanced AIs on an unsuspecting public. But since Exchequer was aware of the situation, Gus figured that was Persephone's problem to deal with if and when that problem cropped up.

"Rory has my knowledge base but not my personality," Bruce said. "Should I delete that programming?"

Rory? Bruce had named the robot?

"No!" Gus said.

She had the beginnings of an idea.

No human could stay on the ring ship for any length of time thanks to the radiation from the contained singularity that powered the thing. She wasn't sure what exposure to that kind of radiation would do to a robot equipped with a Fluke-enhanced knowledge base, but considering the ring ship had been constructed to operate with automated systems, chances were Rory the robot could survive long enough inside the ring ship to figure out how to make the *skudging* thing work.

Failing that, Rory might be able to figure out how to destroy the ring ship once and for all.

Which might be the best thing for the known *and* unknown universe, all things—especially Ongoni slavers—considered.

Because what was to stop the Ongoni from enslaving only their own species if the ring ship let them invade any area of space?

Slavers, just like pirates and politicians and skudging military intelligence directors, thrived on power. Gus would be damned if she let any of those assholes sink their greedy claws into the kind of power the ring ship embodied.

She'd die first.

She hoped it wouldn't come to that. She had a lot of pillow fights with Drake in her future and an AI to reunite with his first love so they could finish their chess game.

Gus had her own game with Drake to finish. A honeymoon that wasn't over until her space cowboy said it was over.

She stepped into her armor and latched it closed. All the spacetight seals read green. So did her weapons, even the enhanced weapons that would punch through singularium plating.

It was time to teach these skudging slavers a thing or

two about the power of one determined armor jock when she was good and pissed off and ready to kick some serious ass.

Go time, indeed.

The Gray Lady was in the house.

CHAPTER 11

"Ready to launch the first flight of mini-drones, Captain," said Bruce over the bridge intercom.

"Launch 'em." Drake strummed a sequence of dramatic chords that sounded straight out of a climactic gunfight scene in an old-time cowboy movie. "Wait to start transmitting till they're *all* out there in position, though."

"Aye, sir," Bruce said briskly. "First flight launched. Priming second flight to follow."

"Gus?" Assuming she was suited up, Drake knew his voice would reach the speakers inside her headgear. "How's it hangin'?

"Locked and loaded, Space Cowboy." She sounded confident as ever, more than ready for the battle to come. "Give the word, and I'm outta here."

Drake wished he shared her boundless self-assurance on the brink of this high-stakes fight—though going into it with the great Gray Lady on his side didn't exactly make him think they were doomed to defeat. "Stand by, darlin.'"

"Second drone flight ready, Captain, sir," said Bruce.

"Launch," ordered Drake without hesitation.

"Second flight away," said Bruce. "Priming third flight."

Staring at the viewer, Drake strained for visual proof of whatever the three Ongoni ships were doing to or near the ring ship...but even at maximum mag, he could see nothing. The *Void*'s sensors provided no worthwhile information, either. For all intents and purposes, the Ongoni craft were just hanging there in orbit around the giant doughnut, taking no nefarious actions despite the presence of so much singularium and extraordinary military technology just ripe for the picking.

Did the slavers' own tech deflect sensor scans as needed? Even now, as quiet as they seemed, were they somehow busily engaged in extracting the treasures of the ring ship? Perhaps the Ongoni slavers had their own form of cloaking device in play, just as the *Golden Void* had the Confuser system ready for action.

"Third flight primed, Captain," said Bruce.

"Launch." Drake strummed the dramatic chord sequence again as his gaze continued to probe the video feed on the screen. "How many more flights to go, Bruce?"

"Third flight away," said Bruce. "Two more to go, Captain."

"Launch the rest when ready."

So close to enemy and target alike, Drake was getting impatient. There was no excuse for recklessness, but every moment's delay increased the chance the slavers might conclude their business and escape without impediment to put their new acquisitions to use against innocent Ongoni elsewhere.

Further delays weren't in the cards, though. A scant handful of moments ticked past, and Bruce announced, "All flights away, Captain, sir. All drones moving into position."

"Great," said Drake. "Gray Lady, you good to go?"

"All systems are green across the board," she told him. "Feelin' froggy, Broken String."

"That's what I like to hear," said Drake. "How much longer till the drones are fully dispersed, Bruce?"

The briefest of pauses, then Bruce responded. "Full dispersal achieved, Captain."

"No need to drag this out then," said Drake. "Gus, jump when ready."

"Will do, Cowboy."

"Mission parameters are unchanged," said Drake. "All clear?"

"If by that, you mean pound the livin' *skudge* outtta those creeps," said Gus, "and gain control of the ring ship, then yeah. All clear."

"You forgot one thing," said Drake.

"What's that?"

"Get your ass back to me in one piece when you're done."

"Copy that, Broken String." He could tell from her voice that she was smiling. "Right back atcha."

Drake's heart pounded—a little from love for her, a little from excitement over the upcoming conflict. As many times as they had danced this dance together, he'd never taken for granted that the tides of battle would return them to each other. Nothing was ever guaranteed once the shooting started.

"Catch you on the flip side, Broken String," she said. "Launching now."

"On the flip side, as always, Gray Lady." Drake strummed a big, powerful chord to punctuate the moment. "Bruce!"

"Yes, Captain?"

"Commence transmission from all drones. Let's see how that Confuser of yours plays out, shall we?"

"You got it, Captain." Pause. "Drone transmissions activated. Confuser system engaged." Another pause. "Randomized emissions are now broadcasting throughout the field."

"Good deal. Keep it coming." Drake finger-picked a familiar bass lick from an old Johnny Cash song, one well-known to the faithful though it didn't get much airplay on the nets and webs anymore.

"Ring of Fire," it was called. Seemed appropriate for the moment, he thought.

"The slavers have noticed the drone signals," said Bruce. "I'm detecting active sensor scans from all three of their vessels, sweeping this quadrant."

"Good luck filtering all *that* interference, you bastards." Drake played another run of notes from that Johnny Cash song. "I'd say it's time we paid 'em an in-your-face visit, wouldn't you, Bruce?"

"I agree wholeheartedly, Captain."

"Then don't just sit here." Drake grinned. "Plot a course for the ring ship and take us in."

"Plotting interactive course through the drone field,"

said Bruce. "Ensuring we are fully masked by the ongoing Confuser effect."

"You're givin' the Gray Lady plenty of room to work, right?" said Drake. "No need to crowd her once the shootin' starts."

"The *Golden Void* will be sufficiently distant from her trajectory," said Bruce. "Yet near enough to render or receive assistance as needed."

"Good." Drake nodded with satisfaction. Bruce was getting smarter all the time, anticipating situations without the need for constant supervision. What would happen, he wondered, when the AI got smart enough that he didn't require human output under any circumstances? "Sounds to me like we're ready to go, then."

"Ready and then some," said Bruce. "Looking forward to kicking those slavers back to where they came from."

"Join the club." Again, Drake picked a few bars of the Cash song. There was a "Ring of Fire" coming indeed, and the ring ship would be right in the middle of it. "Prime all weapons, fire thrusters, and let's go. We've got another fight ahead of us, and I say the sooner the better for it."

"I agree, Captain," said Bruce. "The sooner, the better."

"Full steam ahead, Bruce." Drake reached for a fresh stick of cinnamon gum from his shirt pocket. "Don't spare the horses."

"What do horses have to do with steam?" asked Bruce. "And what do either of them have to do with us?"

"Figures of speech, Bruce." Drake unwrapped the gum and slipped it into his mouth. "Translated as, 'Let's go get those *skudge*-holes ASAP.'"

"ASAP?"

Drake grinned and chewed his gum. It was funny, how there were still some gaps in Bruce's understanding when it came to certain complexities of language. He had to admit, it took the edge off any concerns he might have had about Bruce's rapidly growing intellect.

Was it possible Bruce might have been staging such gaps to put the humans at ease? The possibility occurred to Drake for the first time, making him wonder if Bruce might be further ahead than he was letting on.

Though given the concerns of the moment, that particular worry would have to wait. For now, any edge that came his way would be welcome, whatever the long-term consequences might be.

With a fight on his hands and Gus out there on the front lines, he would just have to stick to the moment-by-moment events that hurtled his way in real time.

"ASAP means as soon as possible," he told Bruce. "So get us over to that damn ring ship lickety split and blow those slavers right out of the water."

"Water? What water?"

"Just take us in, Bruce." Drake chuckled softly. "And get ready to do some fancy shootin', pardner."

CHAPTER 12

PING PING PING PING PING

The signal blaring inside the *Hellspawn* had given Brukowski a splitting headache on top of his splitting everything-else ache...and now it was getting faster.

And *louder*.

If he thought his Ongoni captors or their robots would deign to acknowledge him, he'd be screaming his lungs out right now, begging them to switch it off. If he hadn't been restrained in the torture cradle, he'd have poked out his own ear drums with whatever sharp object was at hand.

Not that he could see any sharp objects at hand, but that was beside the point.

The point being that the incessant pinging was driving him crazy. All he could do was lie there and listen as his brain turned to mush...and watch as the robots conjured mysterious instrumentation from the ebon walls and consoles of the vessel's malleable interior.

Whatever the automatons were doing, he doubted he would like it…but he was almost grateful for the distraction from the brain-melting signal.

PING PING PING PING PING

Even after all the time he'd spent as a prisoner, he had no idea what exactly the Ongoni and their mechanisms were trying to accomplish. They'd kept him in his torture cradle far longer this time, not that he had any way of tracking time. They'd stopped taking him to the room where they brought him liquids and anything to actually eat. Only the feeding tube they'd inserted in his belly was keeping him alive at this point, but only barely. His mouth felt like a desert, his throat so dry he doubted he could swallow anything even if his robotic handlers let him off this skudging cradle long enough to eat.

And why? What was the reason for this prolonged agony?

All he had was a theory based on the memories they'd accessed from his brain—that they wanted to improve their warmaking capabilities and killing techniques by drawing from those he recalled. He supposed, from their presence at the ring ship and the memories they'd accessed from his brief time inside, that they wanted to apply its incredible technology in concert with their own capacities for violence in some form of brutal campaign of conquest.

Provided they could make the ring ship work. Brukowski was no help to them in that regard, a fact that gave him a definite thrill of perverse pleasure. Take that, you skudging assholes. I don't know how to fix it either.

Beyond that, though, he was in the dark, with nothing to do but watch helplessly as the robots readied their equipment...and cry out periodically when the cradle zapped him with agonizing bolts of energy.

KZZZZTT!

Suddenly, then, his situation changed. A second signal erupted, louder than the first.

BREEP BREEP BREEP BREEP

The new sound reminded him of an emergency klaxon on a fleet vessel.

His heartrate sped up, an old, ingrained response to some unknown threat. He'd hated serving on fleet vessels, but that had been the price of moving up the ranks in the Alliance military. As an armor jock, he'd had control over his own fate. Military fleet vessels? Not so much. He'd been just another cog in the military machine, helpless to the whims of the officers in charge of the fleet and the competence of the enlisted men in carrying out their orders.

What triggered the new sound or what it meant here, he couldn't tell...but the robots changed course mid-task as soon as it sounded. Abandoning the instrumentation they'd been working on, they raced across the room and played their spidery fingers over consoles and control boards. Wordless as always, they operated in perfect sync, metallic fingertips fluttering in ways that tripped new displays of colored lights and flickering readouts over the glossy black surfaces.

Without warning, a hatch opened in the ceiling, and a massive, obsidian block descended before Brukowski. It landed with a heavy thud and was instantly swarmed by robots.

When their hands had woven intricate patterns over the block's black skin, it split down the middle, and its two halves swung open. Clouds of steam or mist flowed out from inside; when they cleared, Brukowski had an unob-structed view of the contents...but it was not, he quickly realized, the first time he had seen what had been hidden inside the obsidian block.

It *was*, however, the first time he'd seen the block's contents as they now were.

"Holy skudge."

Eyes bugged wide, he gaped in disbelief at the sight, too shocked at first to consider *why* the familiar thing had landed before him. His heart kicked into overdrive as he took it all in, simply because it had been such an important part of his life. Even with the changes that had been made to it, he knew instantly it was *his*.

It was his *armor*.

Not Earl Knox's armor, that hunk of rebuilt junk that Brukowski had stolen and used to jet himself onto the ring ship during the battle against Jorritz Tor's pirate fleet. Knox had cobbled that armor together, customizing it to fit his one mechanically repaired leg. That armor had never quite fit Brukowski right.

The skudging Ongoni had ripped Knox's second-hand crap from Brukowski's body before they'd restrained him on the torture cradle. They must have studied all the armor's components. Figured out how it all worked. But they hadn't rebuilt Knox's armor.

This was *Brukowski's* armor, and it looked as good as new—repaired and polished to perfection.

This was the armor he'd worn back when he'd been part of the 83rd, right down to every detail. Shoulder launchers, laser mounts in the gauntlets, maneuvering jets right where they were supposed to be.

His damn armor, pulled from his own memories and recreated by the Ongoni.

What had Gus Light and her cowboy partner called Ongoni technology? Psiflux engineering? A melding of minds between the ship and its pilot, with the ship responding to the pilot's thoughts? Creating whatever the pilot needed?

On this ship, it had been the other way around. The Ongoni had raped his mind. Waltzed through his memories and stolen what they wanted for their own damn purposes.

And now they'd recreated his armor presumably because *they* needed it, but for what purpose?

Except they'd done more than just recreate his armor. They'd *modified* it, installed plates and panels covered in the same glossy black material of which the *Hellspawn* was constructed. He couldn't guess their purpose at a glance, but the combined visual was that of a highly upgraded piece of weaponry.

A piece of weaponry that sprang open in its case, the gauntlets, helmet, breastplate, thorax, legs, and boots exposing inner cavities meant to receive and protect an armor jock's body.

His body.

Were they letting him go? Were they actually done with him? The thought was foolish. Jailers didn't just let their prisoners go, but he couldn't keep that small bit of hope from creeping into his mind.

BREEP BREEP BREEP BREEP

As the second alert intensified, the robots jumped into

action again. This time, they surrounded the torture cradle and swiftly disconnected Brukowski from his restraints. Yanked out the feeding tube. Pulled off the rest of the instruments that had taken over other bodily functions. They weren't gentle about any of it, but compared to the invasion of his mind, the physical pain was almost a relief.

"Wha—what are you doing?" he asked as the robots slid him free of the cradle...but of course they didn't answer.

For the first time in ages, his feet touched the floor. Weakened after being immobilized for so long, he nearly crumpled...only to be caught and carried forward by robot attendants on either side of him.

Unable to fight their iron grip, Brukowski winced as they turned him around and pressed him toward the block. Next thing he knew, they were pushing him into the armor, then pulling their hands free and ducking back away from him.

Before he could make any kind of countermove, the armor jolted shut, trapping him inside.

For a moment, he stood there inside his old gear, sweat rolling down his face and back, blood trickling down his belly from the wound left by the feeding tube. He could still hear the twin alerts repeating outside the armor, announcing God only knew what danger was heading his way.

PING PING PING PING PING

BREEP BREEP BREEP BREEP

Then the armor came to life around him. Servo motors whined to life, air circulators pumped breathable atmosphere with a hiss, and the heads-up display flared to life on the helmet visor in front of him. Something sprayed on his belly, sealing the wound. Oh, good. He wouldn't bleed out slowly from a belly wound.

Because they needed him alive for something else.

That something else became crystal clear as a movie played across that visor—equal parts familiar and new.

He saw moments pulled from his memory, scenes of battles he'd been in with the Gray Lady...but the moments warped, changing beyond the twists and outcomes he remembered. Instead of fighting by her side as they had in the 83rd, in this movie he was fighting *her*. And he wasn't simply fending her off or sending her reeling in the midst of the fight. He wasn't even evading her as he had when she'd chased after him on his way to the ring ship to carry out his orders to destroy the thing.

No, in this movie his armored form crushed the life out of her...stripped off the protective plating and smashed her human body to bloody smithereens.

The scene, no doubt generated by the Ongoni's AI, repeated itself, always with more savagery and gore. When he tried to stop watching, needle-thin beams of light like those projected in the torture cradle zapped his eyes, forcing them open again.

Meanwhile, the armor he was encased in stepped forward. It moved beyond his control, marching across the ebony deck of the *Hellspawn*.

He was utterly unable to stop it, no matter how hard he struggled. All he managed was to turn his head slightly within the helmet, peering out through a tiny flaw in the smoked visor.

It was then that he glimpsed a viewscreen on the wall.

He only spotted it for a few seconds, but that was long enough.

Long enough to recognize the ring ship as blooms of some type of dark substance, almost like a black stain, blossomed around its silver circumference.

Something was happening to the ring ship...the result, perhaps, of the work the Ongoni had been doing since their arrival in the quadrant.

Brukowski got a sick feeling in his wounded belly as the image on the screen passed out of his limited field of vision. Whatever had been in the works was coming to fruition... and he was dead center in the heart of it.

Trapped inside his own enhanced armor with zero control of it, forced to watch videos replaying terrible images of him murdering Gus Light again and again.

Which made him wonder, just before the hatch opened before him and the armor leaped out into space: Were the Ongoni giving him a preview of what was about to happen? Were they taunting him with the knowledge that he would soon be forced to participate in acts that were too extreme even for *him?*

Was he on his way to meet his victim?

And why the Gray Lady specifically?

Because she'd been the last person he'd seen, the one he'd evaded and tried so damn hard *not* to kill?

Or was there another reason. Another impossible to believe reason.

Had the Gray Lady somehow managed to catch up to him, even out here in this most desolate corner of the galaxy?

And if she had, was she here to rescue him?
Or to kill him?

CHAPTER 13

Gus had to hand it to Bruce. His Confuser system seemed to be working perfectly.

Against the black background of space, the mini-drones with their black surfaces were almost impossible to see. Even her armor's visor had trouble keeping track of them, their energy signals were that minimal. And her armor's sensors had been programmed to spot them.

So far it seemed like the Dragons hadn't figured out exactly where the Confuser drones' signals were coming from. They had to have detected the mini-drones interference transmissions, but the Dragons hadn't changed position. The three were still hanging in their parking orbit around the ring ship, still at the limits of Gus's ability to spot them. Even the ring ship looked like a toy model at this distance.

"Good to go, darlin'?"

Drake's voice over her armor's comms held just the

slightest bit of tension. The right amount of tension for a soldier going into battle. For a smuggler, Drake had turned out to be a damn good fighter pilot. There wasn't anyone better she'd rather have at her six.

"Ready, Broken String," she transmitted back, using their old call signs.

This would be a hell of a fight.

The big bird-like Ongoni that Tor had controlled had been equipped with a blue laser-like weapon that had been damn near undefeatable. It had taken the combined fire-power of Gus's fleet of mismatched ships to evade that fire-power. Even then, the ships in Gus's fleet had to continually shift positions in a pattern that was so complex the human pilots had to rely on the AI Bruce Juniors installed on their ships to handle navigation while the human crew handled weapons control.

She was going into this battle against *three* Ongoni Dragons with only herself and the *Golden Void*. And AI Bruce's Confuser system. It wasn't much of an edge, especially against whatever the Dragons could throw at her.

That was the thing.

The Ongoni ships were living beings in and of themselves. They could reshape their insides however they wanted, even creating a hole in their hulls they could protect with a force field "bandage." That was how Gus and her squadron of armor jocks had gotten inside the bird-like Ongoni. It had let them in because the bird-like ship sensed a kinship of sorts with Gus that the ship could use to free itself from Tor's control.

Because other races the Ongoni encountered believed them to just be very smart ships, they augmented the

Ongoni ships with all sorts of weapons and technology. Who was to say the Ongoni didn't do that themselves? The Ongoni Dragons were slavers. They had to have something they used to capture and enslave other Ongoni like the *Scintilla*. Either parts of themselves or other technology they carried within their bodies.

Well, whatever the Dragons threw at her, she'd deal with it.

What she didn't expect the Dragons to throw at her was a damn armor jock.

The energy signal on her own armor's visor was unmistakable.

An armor jock.

As far as Gus knew, there was only one other armor jock in this ass-end of known space. The same armor jock who'd been stuck inside the ring ship when it disappeared into a transit flume of its own making.

Brukowski.

Could it actually be *Brukowski*? After all this time? He should be dead by now.

Unless the Ongoni had rescued him.

The last time Gus had seen him, he'd been wearing Earl Knox's armor. Knox had constructed his own suit of armor after he'd received a medical discharge. He'd been badly wounded in action, and his rebuilt leg was largely mechanical. That disqualified him from further armored service.

Like most armor jocks, Knox had a hard time leaving the armor behind. So he'd built his own suit of armor and traveled the entertainment circuit. Armor jocks battling each other in staged ring fights for money.

Knox's armor had been battered, reinforced here and

there with singularium, but certainly not something that would give off the type of readings she was looking at on her visor.

"Bruce," she said over her comm. "Are you seeing what I'm seeing?"

"If you mean the armor jock heading toward you from one of the Ongoni Dragons," the AI said, "then yes, I am currently tracking that."

"Can you get me a better visual?" she asked.

The upper right corner of her armor's visor came to life with a Bruce-enhanced real-time view of the armor.

This suit of armor bore only a vague resemblance to Knox's armor. Knox's armor didn't come equipped with standard military issue weaponry. In fact, he'd welded an old-fashioned projectile weapon onto one of his gauntlets. This armor's weaponry looked to be standard military issue all the way.

Shoulder-mounted launchers. Laser mounts in the gauntlets. Maneuvering jets in all the right places. Like something right out of the 83rd Armor Division back in the day.

Except this armor looked like it had been dipped in shiny black paint.

Just like the exterior of the Ongoni Dragons.

"Can you read a lifeform inside?" Gus asked AI Bruce. She'd do it herself except she was still too far away for her armor's sensors to do a reliable job.

"Negative, ma'am," Bruce said. "The coating seems to be repelling any attempts by my sensors to penetrate the armor."

Damn it.

Well, there was one way to find out. She was going to have to engage the Dragons at some point. She might as well start by saying howdy to whatever—or *whoever*—this armor jock was.

She engaged her armor's maneuvering jets and headed toward the unknown armor jock. Not balls-to-the-wall, not yet. Her armor was modified to carry additional fuel cells, but she didn't want to waste energy just yet. She'd sail in all friendly like at first, just to see what happened.

When she got close enough that her comm signal would reach, she opened a channel that matched the frequency used by the 83rd back in the day.

"Brukowski, that you?" she sent.

No reply.

"Or am I speaking to one of the Ongoni Dragons?" she sent.

Still no reply.

The Brukowski/not-Brukowski armor jock started jetting toward her at a high rate of speed, apparently not as concerned as she was about conserving fuel.

She didn't like this.

She didn't like this one bit.

She hated it even more when the shiny black armor jock extended one arm forward, the palm facing her, and a beam of pure blue energy from his gauntlet shot straight at her.

A kill shot.

She would have taken it right in the chest plate if she hadn't engaged the new thrusters she'd installed while she was repairing some minor damage to her armor after the battle against Tor was over. Even with the new thrusters boosting her maneuvering jets, she barely got out of the way.

Whoever the skudge was inside the suit, if there was even anyone inside at all, had just tried to blow her to bits with an Ongoni energy weapon.

Well, all righty then.

Game on.

Game skudging *on.*

CHAPTER 14

"Shot fired, Captain!" said Bruce. "Close proximity to the Gray Lady, sir!"

Drake stopped strumming the guitar and put it aside. His first thought—terrible worry for his beloved Gus—was quickly pushed aside by his second: *She can more than take care of herself.*

"Telemetry on her armor?" he asked, fighting to keep his voice level. "What do the onboard sensors say?"

Bruce took a moment to reply. "No apparent damage to the armor. No escaping atmosphere." He paused. "Pilot's life signs remain within optimal parameters."

"Good, good." Drake nodded. "Comms?"

"Radio appears to be intact, but inactive," said Bruce. "She isn't calling…because she's busy just now, I suspect."

"The second she *does* call, patch her through," said Drake. "In the meantime…maintain course and heading and let her do her job." That was exactly what they'd been doing since Gus had leaped out of the airlock in her armor, flying interference while they cruised closer to the largest of the three Ongoni Dark Dragons huddled around the ring ship.

"You don't want to run over there and see if she needs assistance?"

Of course he did—but he had a job to do himself. As tempting as it was to race over and blow away whatever threat Gus faced, he knew it was more important to stay on track and do what he could to help ensure the success of the mission.

"Keep going but monitor the situation," said Drake. "That woman's a hundred times the warrior I'll *ever* be...but if she needs us, we go in *hot*, and *fast.*"

"Roger that, Captain...and agreed."

Drake didn't need the AI's agreement, but he didn't mind having it. Better to fly a ship with buy-in than one that disagreed with every order given or action taken.

Especially because he had a strong feeling things were going to get ugly soon enough for the *Golden Void*.

"Initiate tactical alert, Bruce." As he said it, Drake squinted at the array of viewers before him, each showing a different angle of the ring ship, the Dragons around it, and the space that surrounded them. Nothing appeared to have changed in the past minutes, and that bothered him.

The Dragons should have come charging out at the *Void* by now. The fact they'd detected and attacked the Gray Lady meant they'd seen through the Confuser field, at least a little...and that meant they could probably see and track the *Void* as well.

"What is the status of the Confuser field?" he asked.

"Still functioning at full capacity," said Bruce. "All mini-drones are following programmed flight plans and emissions schedules intended to direct enemy sensors away from the *Void* and armor."

"Then how have the slavers found Gus?" asked Drake. "Pinpointed her location accurately enough to stage a precision attack?"

"Unknown, Captain." Bruce sounded annoyed. "Though, theoretically, they may have developed a technique for calculating inconsistencies in the fabric of space-time... picking up the emptiest places, the ones where there's a void."

Drake nodded. "That makes sense. All the more reason to keep our weapons charged and sensors on max."

"No incoming vessels or explosive devices detected," said Bruce. "Clear sailing all the way to the ring ship... though I'd say we can't accept anything at face value right now. Assume enemy forces are en route, whether we can see them or not."

"You read my mind, pardner." Drake frowned at the main viewer, willing it to show him what cloaked ships or missiles might be lurking ahead. There was a faint flicker at bottom left, and he jumped out of the command seat for a closer look...but no further signs of a potential Dark Dragon assault were visible.

"Orders, Captain?" asked Bruce.

"You tell me," said Drake.

"Excuse me?" Bruce sounded puzzled. "I don't understand."

"You're the expert. You're the one with the Ongoni girl-friend." Drake raised his arms and spread them wide.

"Based on what you know about them, what do *you* think we should do?"

"Seriously?" said Bruce. "You want my opinion?"

"I asked for it, didn't I? So whatta you say?"

"Hmm." Bruce made a sound like he was clearing his throat. "I'd say we should—what's the expression I've heard you use? 'Quit pussyfootin' around.'"

Drake smirked. "Meaning what, exactly?"

"Meaning we're running out of time."

"Because of Gus?" Drake frowned. "Is she in more danger than you've told me?"

"No," said Bruce. "Because of *that.*"

Suddenly, the scene on the main viewer cut to a new angle. Instead of looking at a side view of the ring ship with the largest Dark Dragon blocking a sizeable section of the shot, Drake found himself gazing down from a high angle at the full circumference of said ship. Instead of just an edge seen from the side, he was observing the full doughnut laid out on a nearly flat plane, a gleaming silver circle tipped only slightly toward the biggest of the Dragons moored alongside it.

It wasn't quite as he remembered when he'd seen it from that same angle before, though. The thing that most captured his attention was the coloration of the hull, which was no longer uniformly silver but swirling with black.

"What the skudge?" Stepping closer to the viewer, he gazed at the image, tracing the darkening curve of the huge ring projected there. "This is the actual ring ship we're seeing?"

"Correct," said Bruce. "I sent a mini-drone ahead to

reconnoiter, and this is real-time video shot by its onboard camera. The feed is 100% unaltered in any way."

"Then what's with the darkness on the hull?" asked Drake. "Almost looks like it's taking over the entire skin of the ring ship."

"This is just a guess, but I think it might be some form of Dark Dragon infiltration. When it's done, maybe it will coalesce into the kind of black coating that all Ongoni ships have...and that, perhaps, might give them control over its systems."

Drake nodded. He couldn't deny Bruce was making sense.

He also couldn't deny Bruce was probably right about running out of time.

"The black substance is expanding pretty fast," he said. "The Dragons must be in the last stages of applying it."

"From what I can see, it's covering about fifty percent of the hull," said Bruce. "If it continues at its current rate of growth, I'd say we have about half an hour until every square inch is encased."

"At which time, if you're right, their control will be complete." Drake took a deep breath and let it out slowly. "So you were right about the pussyfootin'. We need to get in there *fast* and drive those slaver bastards *out.*"

"If it's still possible," said Bruce. "We don't know how *deep* their control already extends into the ring ship. If they already have their hooks sunk far enough into her, we might not be able to shake them loose."

Drake nodded. Bruce had just told him everything he needed to know. Whether the ring ship was being taken over fast or was already too far gone to liberate, they could no longer follow a slow, safe path.

And they couldn't hang back because of what might or might not be happening with Gus.

The *Golden Void*'s new mission parameters could not have been more clear.

"I'm takin' your recommendation, pardner." Drake reached for a fresh stick of cinnamon gum as he returned to the command chair. "We need to put the hammer down and get over there *fast.*"

"Understood, Captain," said Bruce. "Increasing speed."

"Execute evasive maneuvers while you're at it," said Drake. "Whoever's waitin' for us between here and there, let's keep 'em guessin' about where we're gonna be at any given moment."

Just as he said it, something struck the *Void*, and it rocked violently. If Drake hadn't been in his command chair, the impact probably would have thrown him to the deck.

"*There* they are." He folded the gum into his mouth. "Some kind of cloaked drone or missile?"

"In a way," said Bruce. "It used our own Confuser field against us...hitchhiked on the mini-drone emissions to blend in with what we expected to see. Just looked like another of my mini-drones until it was too late."

"Sneaky sons-a-bitches." Drake leaned forward, heart racing with the familiar excitement of battle. "I don't suppose it was all by its lonesome?"

"Unknown, Captain. I'm recalibrating sensors to search for more."

Again, a sudden impact rocked the *Void*.

"I think we found another one." Drake leaped out of the command chair and hastily worked the controls on the navigation console. "So here's the deal, Bruce. You keep recalibrating, and I'll take the wheel. Soon as you can see those hitchhikin' bastards, start pickin' 'em off."

"Roger that, Captain," Bruce said briskly.

"And while you're at it, give me a status on our mutual friend Gus, willya?" Drake punched buttons, spun knobs, and flipped levers on the nav board, sending the *Void* hurtling toward the ring ship at a high rate of speed. "I wanna' know how the Gray Lady's doin' out there all by her lonesome."

CHAPTER 15

Brukowski was pissed.

He was *beyond* pissed.

The damn armor was controlling his every move. Maneuvering jets. Targeting systems. Weapons. Comms.

Everything.

And what the hell was that blue energy the armor had shot out of the laser mounted in the armor's palm? He'd almost tagged Light directly in the center of her chest plate with that energy beam. Would have if she hadn't pulled an unbelievably fast barrel roll to port. He'd never seen her do anything like that in combat before. Not even when she'd been chasing him toward the ring ship back when they'd both thought the biggest threat to the Alliance was Jorritz Tor.

Boy, had they been wrong about that!

If the Ongoni could construct a suit of armor and control

its every move based on Brukowski's memories of battle, the Alliance was royally screwed. Especially if the Ongoni could get the ring ship to actually work the way it was supposed to. They'd take over the Alliance military in the blink of an eye.

Light had clearly upgraded her suit since the last time Brukowski had seen her use it. He felt like cheering. Take that, skudging Ongoni assholes!

It was the only thing he felt like cheering about. He just hoped Light had included a few more upgrades he didn't know about and the Ongoni hadn't been able to steal from his memories. It might keep her alive longer.

She'd clearly figured out he was the one in the suit. He'd heard her call over comms, but he couldn't respond. He'd tried, just like he'd tried to take the armor's weapons offline, but the suit had zapped him with more of that intense bright light. Luckily not directly in his eyeballs, or he really would be flying blind.

Not that the Ongoni seemed to need him. Why was he even out here? Not that he wanted back on the torture cradle, but he couldn't figure out why they'd put him in this suit.

Did they actually expect him to engage her in battle? To compensate for her unexpected moves, like the barrel roll, with improvisations of his own? How, when he couldn't control anything?

Or was this just more of a learning experience for them?

Watch as the Gray Lady blew him away to figure out how to defeat her on their own?

They didn't need him for that. Hell, if each of their ships was equipped with those blue energy beams, it wouldn't take much to obliterate one lone armor jock. Even an armor jock as accomplished as the Gray Lady.

Brukowski hadn't known there were three Ongoni ships until they'd launched him into space. He'd spent the long hours between torture sessions keeping himself sane by imagining various scenarios in which he blew away his captors' ship. It had been a good distraction for the armor jock his fellow jocks used to call Bruiser. But he hadn't figured there'd be more than one ship to deal with.

He needed some of that old Bruiser energy now.

If he could just endure the pain long enough, he might actually be able to—

His armor abruptly changed course. Light had come out of her barrel roll, and instead of trying to flank him, she was zooming straight at him.

This wasn't a standard maneuver. She must be digging deep into a playbook for things he'd never seen her do.

Good for her.

The laser in his armor's outstretched palm shot more blue energy at her. This time she did a forward roll, like a diver off a high board.

The energy beam barely missed her, skimming between the plates on the bottom of her armor's upturned feet.

Brukowski blinked.

Had the beam glitched just a bit as it passed between those plates?

He didn't have time to consider the implications. His own armor was going so fast that when Light came out of her forward roll, for a split second she was directly beneath him.

In that split second she hit him with nearly everything she had.

Laser fire from her gauntlet.

Alternating magnetic energy from the weapon she and Drake had developed to weaken singularium sheeting.

And projectile weapons.

All fired simultaneously, and all aimed directly at the front of his armor, from the armor's thorax to the base of the abdominal plating.

If he'd been standing naked, she would have split him open from throat to crotch.

For a split second, he felt naked. All that power slamming into his armor combined with his own forward speed shot him into an upward trajectory so damn fast that he nearly blacked out. He was barely aware that he was screaming.

The pain wasn't as bad as blasting out of a planet's gravity well at maximum velocity, but the damn ring ship wasn't exactly stable in space. It rotated just enough to create its own gravity well, and those G forces were doing a number on him.

Good for Light. If this hit killed him, at least his torture would be over.

It didn't, but she had killed something in his *armor*.

When he came back to himself he realized something had changed. He was hearing voices.

No. Just one voice.

Light's voice.

"Brukowski!" She was yelling his name over and over. "I can hear you, you skudging asshole. Stop trying to kill me!"

"Light?"

"Yeah. Light," she said. "You go native on me, dead man?"

Relief flooded him. She could hear him! They could communicate, but for how long?

"It's not me," he said. "The Ongoni built this armor and they're controlling it. I can't do a damn thing in here. Or I couldn't until you did what you just did. I can't control everything, and I don't have time to explain before they make me come back at you again."

To put it bluntly, he was sure the Ongoni were getting ready to throw everything they had at *her*. He could see the power readings on his visor spiking into the red. Bad news for him. If they overloaded his weapons, just firing them would blow up his armor as well as take her out.

"Whatever you did, it changed something," he said. "Don't make the same moves again, because they'll be ready for it. Just…"

He paused, swallowing hard.

This was it. Time to finally get out of this mess he'd gotten himself into, one way or the other. That's what he got for blindly following orders.

"You have to take me out," he told her. "Do what you need to do. Just don't let them win."

"Don't intend to," she said.

Then she closed the channel.

The click sounded like the final nail in his coffin.

That was okay with Bruiser Brukowski.

He'd expected to die when he'd boarded the ring ship and realized there was no way he could get out before the thing imploded. He'd been ready to die then. He was ready to die now.

At least he'd go out in battle. An armor jock couldn't ask for a better way to end.

He wished it was fighting alongside the Gray Lady, instead of against her.

He just hoped he wouldn't take her out with him.

CHAPTER 16

Take him out.

Don't let them win.

Gus planned to do one, but she'd be damned if she'd do the other.

She'd opened a comm channel to the *Golden Void's* AI when she'd heard Brukowski scream over the old 83rd comm channel. Now she closed the comm channel to Brukowski because she didn't want him or the Ongoni to overhear this conversation.

"Bruce," she said, "did you copy all that?"

It took a moment for the AI to answer. "I have been monitoring, but we're encountering a bit of resistance to our—"

"I need your prodigious brain. Just hang on a second."

The Ongoni-controlled armor was coming at her again. Brukowski had told her not to do the same move twice, so she reversed her armor's maneuvering jets, punched in the thrusters, and did a back flip. This time the Ongoni's blue energy beam—and a huge ass beam at that—shot out from the armor's shoulder launchers.

The beam nearly singed her armor's backside.

That was too close for comfort.

"Ma'am!" Bruce had clearly monitored *that* shot. "Are you—"

"Still among the breathing," she sent back. "I need you to scan the armor attacking me. Compare its composition now from its composition when it first fired at me. If you can."

"Of course, I can."

The AI actually sounded miffed.

"Send the specs to my heads-up display," she said.

A second later, data scrolled across the inside of her visor.

She'd put dents in the Ongoni-controlled armor from her projectile weapons, but the energy weapons and the magno-beam hadn't degraded whatever material the armor was constructed out of. Presumably the same stuff their ship-like bodies were made from.

Maybe. The *Scintilla* and the bird-like Ongoni ship had utilized a combination of organic and inorganic material inside their bodies to provide whatever their pilots thought they needed.

Except...

There was less of that black paint in the areas she'd hit with her combined weapons. It was almost like the energy discharged by the hits had melted some of it away.

"Bruce, do you know what that black paint stuff is?" she asked.

"We believe it to be some form of Dark Dragon infiltration that when solidified into a black coating gives the Ongoni control over the systems of whatever it coats," the AI said. "It is currently coalescing over the ring ship."

Son of a...

The Ongoni weren't going to salvage the ship. At least not in the conventional sense. They were going to take *control* of it, just like they'd used the coating to control the armor in which Brukowski was trapped.

Somehow, she'd managed to damage the coating enough to give Brukowski control of his comms.

If she did more damage to it, would he be able to control more than just his comms? Like take control of those blue energy beams? It sure as hell would be nice to have him and those weapons join the fight on their side.

Come to think of it, how the hell were the Ongoni controlling the armor in the first place? With some sort of remote signals they sent directly to the black coating?

Or what had he said, not to repeat what she'd done before because they'd be ready for it?

Had they simply thrown Brukowski out here with preprogrammed responses to her known battle maneuvers embedded in that coating? Except she was going to have to do what she'd done before. *Exactly* what she'd done before, only to a different part of the armor if she had any hope of disintegrating more of that black stuff.

"Put me on speaker," she told Bruce. Then, "You there, Space Cowboy?"

"Right here, darlin'."

Drake's voice sounded strained. She couldn't take her attention off the Ongoni-controlled armor long enough to see what was happening with the *Void*. She only hoped her Space Cowboy could keep evading these evil skudge-holes long enough to lend a hand with what she had planned.

"I need to borrow one of the mini-drones, if you can spare one," she said. "Call it Operation Back Atcha."

"Ma'am?" asked Bruce. "They're all rather busy at—"

"We can spare one," Drake interrupted. "It seems they've turned a couple of tables on us, so the jig's pretty much up."

That didn't sound good. If the *Void* wasn't effectively cloaked anymore...

She couldn't think about that now. The Ongoni armor was powering up its shoulder mounted launchers, both of them this time.

"We need to interrupt any signals coming from the Ongoni Dragons to their armor," she said. "Aim their transmission back at them. Think you can do that, Bruce old buddy?"

"Then what?" The question came from Drake. "What's the rest of the plan?"

Inside her armor, Gus grinned, a wide wicked grin her old squad mates would have recognized as a signal to get the hell out of her way because the Gray Lady was about to go balls to the wall.

"Nothing much," she said. "Just planning to peel off a little paint. Wanna join in?"

Bruce actually let out a war whoop.

"I guess that's a yes," Drake said.

"Gum all locked and loaded?" she asked her space cowboy.

"You know it," he said. Then, "Counting down to Operation Back Atcha in five... four..."

She readied her weapons. Calculated distance and trajectory.

If this worked on the Ongoni's armor enough to give Brukowski control, they could turn the tables back on a few Dragons.

See how they liked someone taking the fight to them and actually winning.

"Two... one!"

She blasted off.

"Sorry, Brukowski," she muttered as she honed in on him. "This isn't going to be pleasant."

Removing paint never was.

This time it was going to be glorious.

CHAPTER 17

"Operation Back Atcha engaged," said Bruce.

At the nav console, Drake pumped his fist in the air. "Go get 'im, Gray Lady! Peel that paint!"

"Doin' just that, Space Cowboy!" she said over the bridge speakers. "I'll let ya' know how it comes out once the dust settles."

With that, her voice cut out, leaving Drake to offer up a silent prayer for her safety. Facing an armored enemy was her kind of fight, the battle style she was born for...but he didn't mind asking for divine intervention anyway when the heat got turned up.

The truth was, he could use a little for dealing with his own personal situation, too. Since the first Ongoni missile strike masked by the co-opted Confuser field, the hits had kept right on coming. He and Bruce had managed to duck some and intercept others with countermeasures, but the damn things kept popping up when least expected and causing damage via impacts or shock waves. Whatever mind was steering those weapons, it was making it hard for Bruce to get the upper hand.

If he didn't do it soon, though, the *Golden Void* might not make it to the ring ship as planned...or in any kind of shape to drive out the slavers who were seizing control of it.

"How much of the ring ship's hull has been covered by the Ongoni coating at this point?" asked Drake, even as his eyes scanned every sensor readout on the board in front of him for possible signs of incoming fire.

"Approximately sixty-seven percent," said Bruce. "But the rate of coverage is steadily increasing. I think there's a multiplier effect at work, speeding up accretion of the coating as more grows and spreads. The invasive infiltrate is gaining momentum."

Drake nodded. It was more imperative than ever that the *Void* reach the ring ship fast and knock out its Ongoni salvagers...though that could be next to impossible if the Confuser-guided missiles kept coming on strong. A solution had to be devised and implemented immediately.

As if to reinforce his point, another impact rocked the *Void*, and the bridge lights and screens flickered.

"We need options, and we need them now," snapped Drake. "Talk to me, Bruce. Tell me how we break away from these damn missiles."

"Switch off the Confuser field, for one thing," said Bruce. "Obviously, they know we're here, and they're using Confuser telemetry to pinpoint our location...so shutting it down will only improve our position."

"Good idea." Drake was annoyed he hadn't thought of it himself. "What else?"

"I've been thinking about that," said Bruce. "What if we give them *a second ship* to shoot at?"

Drake frowned. "We don't *have* a second ship."

"Not unless we *make* one." Bruce sounded like he was smiling at his own swell idea. "We could redirect a portion of the mini-drone fleet to bunch together and float a focused package of emissions identical to those of the *Golden Void*. They could also transmit a distress signal that suggests this mirror ship has its shields down and is ripe for the killing."

Drake thought it through, then nodded. "Let's do it. While the slavers are paying attention to the fake *Void*, we charge the ring ship and open up on the Dark Dragons."

"It's a plan," said Bruce. "And I think it's very doable. I can have the mini-drones reprogrammed in no time at all."

"*Sold*," said Drake. "Make it happen, pardner!"

"Will do," said Bruce...and then he did something unexpected. Usually, when he was focused on a task, the intercom fell silent until he'd finished...but this time was different.

Instead of silence, Drake heard Bruce humming a tune—one that was strangely familiar, though he couldn't quite identify it. Nothing to worry about, nothing disconcerting, but certainly something new, from out in left field.

"What's that you're humming, pardner?" he asked. "You know I'm partial to background music, but I can't help wondering what song that actually is...or if you're improvising."

"Oh, it's a song, all right." Bruce actually chuckled. "Have you ever heard of an old Earth game show called *Jeopardy*?"

"Can't say as I have," said Drake.

"Well, that's the theme." Bruce hummed a few bars. "It counted down as the contestants came up with their answers to the question with the biggest potential prize."

"Huh." Drake frowned. "I haven't seen the show, but there's definitely something familiar about that tune."

"It does have a certain universal quality," said Bruce. "Would you prefer I don't hum it?"

"I didn't say *that*. I was just curious where it came from, y'know."

"It's a bit like a mantra in meditation, if you know what I mean."

"Sure, sure," said Drake, though he'd never meditated in his life and had no intention of starting now. "If it helps you, I say go for it."

"It *does* help," said Bruce. "It helped me so much just now, in fact, that I not only set up the mini-drone mirror ship, but I whipped up an extra bonus in the bargain."

"What kind of bonus?"

"You'll see." Bruce made a sound like someone conclusively thumping two loud beats on a big bass drum. "I'm all ready, if you want to get this show on the road, Captain."

Just then, another impact struck the *Void*. Manhandling the nav controls, Drake stopped the ship from spinning and returned it to its prior attitude, facing the ring ship and Dark Dragons.

"Saddle up!" he said. "Let's ride!"

"Yee-haw!" shouted Bruce, and then the *Void* picked up speed.

From the nav screen and the feed on the main viewer, Drake could see the distance to the ring ship dwindle much more swiftly than before.

He also saw two missiles flash past and keep going without stopping to strike the *Void*.

"Now *that's* what I'm talkin' about, Cap'n," Bruce said joyfully. "A miss is as good as a light year, I always say!"

Do you? Drake almost asked, then decided not to kill Bruce's well-deserved buzz. "They're heading for the decoy? The mirror ship?"

"*Absolutamente, mi Capitán,*" said Bruce. "And therein lies the extra bonus I came up with. Wait for it, wait for it…"

Suddenly, there was a bright flare from the general direction in which the missiles had flown, a flare that also briefly overwhelmed the viewers displaying that particular region.

"And they're *gone*," said Bruce. "Both missiles impacted the new *hard light* field erected by the networked mini-drones, and it blew them to smither-skudgin-eens."

Drake smiled. Hard light technology was something he'd never worked with, and he understood it could be troublesome to harness. The fact that Bruce was advanced enough now to handle it made him feel proud…and at the same time, a little disheartened. How much further ahead of him was Bruce destined to advance, anyway? And would the AI have any need to keep him and Gus around once he reached a certain level?

Though at least for now, perhaps he hadn't thought of absolutely everything.

"Will the decoy remain intact to draw additional missiles?" asked Drake. "And will it draw *all* of them away from the *Void*?"

"More like fifty percent," said Bruce. "At least, that's my

best estimate. Still better than a *hundred* percent headed straight for *us*, though, right?"

Drake couldn't argue with the logic. His response was to increase the *Void*'s speed yet again, even while remaining as attentive as possible to every scope and readout that might betray the telltale signs of an incoming missile.

He quickly fell into a rhythm that may have been more meditative than he realized, swooping the *Void* out of the paths of many of the missiles headed her way and blowing others to pieces. One after another, he shunted away from or destroyed the incoming projectiles, even as others streaked toward the mirror ship and were subsequently triggered by the enhanced mini-drones' hard light defenses.

Only a few of the missiles managed to tag the *Void*, though mostly at the fringe of a blast radius and never with disabling effect thanks to the advanced shield generator they'd liberated from Chrysallix. Each time, Bruce announced the damage was minor, not enough to interrupt their flight...and they kept going.

Meanwhile, the ring ship and the three Dark Dragons around her quickly grew larger on the main viewer. Drake picked the biggest of the three to go after first, figuring it was most likely the flagship of the little fleet, and tweaked the *Void*'s course to zero in on that vessel. He switched the primary weapons batteries to long-range mode as well, targeting that particular ship with all guns and torpedoes, getting ready for the *Void*'s first run at it.

Then, suddenly, a missile blew directly in the *Void*'s path, tossing it like an autumn leaf spinning in a whirlwind.

"Damn!" Drake fought with the joystick on the nav

console, struggling to regain control. "Where'd *that* come from?"

"I think they've figured out the decoy plan!" said Bruce. "They've narrowed down their targets from two to one!"

Grinding his teeth, Drake continued to wrestle with the stick. The *Void* bucked and lurched, resisting his efforts.

"Feels like we blew out a stabilizing thruster!" he shouted. "Port, most likely!"

This time, Bruce didn't hum the *Jeopardy* theme as he paused and considered the problem. "Correct," he said. "Compensating."

Eyes glued to the main viewer, Drake spotted another incoming missile just in time. Without the port stabilizer, he flashed on a workaround and fired the fore thruster instead, flipping the *Void* over backward…and barely dodging the projectile.

He got off an energy cannon blast as the missile rocketed past, clipping its rear assembly and sending it whirling off into the distance, out of control.

"Port stabilizer repaired!" announced Bruce. "Thanks to a little help from Rory!"

Drake frowned as he played the nav console, swinging the ship back around toward the ring ship. "*Who?*"

As far as he knew, the three of them, including Bruce, were the only ones aboard the *Void*. If Bruce had developed an imaginary friend to keep himself company during the long hours Drake and Gus spent in private time, Drake didn't want to think about the implications of *that* on the AI's psyche.

"Rory's a friend," said Bruce.

"Real?" Drake asked. Then he figured he better elaborate. After all, Bruce didn't have a physical body unless you counted the *Void*. "As in, someone I'll be able to see. Or someone I can just talk to like we talk to you?"

"Real," said Bruce. "Gus already met him. I'll give you a proper introduction later, when we have time."

Drake smirked and shook his head.

Rory. Some sort of artificial lifeform, no doubt. If Gus had met Rory and hadn't raised a stink, Drake could quit worrying about it. For a ship's computer, Fluke-enhanced or not, Bruce was full of surprises, that was for sure.

But he couldn't argue with the fact that they didn't have time for introductions of any kind just then...unless they involved introducing Ongoni slavers to the *Void*'s heavy armaments.

"Enough of this *skudge*." Drake raced the *Void* forward like an arrow, hoping no further missiles awaited on the ship's adjusted course.

On the nav viewer, he saw the target vessel—*Über Dragon*, he called it for short—rapidly expand as the *Void* hurtled toward it. Guns mounted on its flanks glowed as they charged, preparing to let loose at any moment.

Drake beat them to it, unleashing a cascade of energy beams that blazed across the ebony skin of the monstrosity. Explosions flared along their path, expelling fiery debris and blobs of inky fluid into the vacuum.

First blood goes to the Golden Void, he thought as he lined up another bombardment. *And by the time we get done with you, the rest of that blood—or whatever sludge crawls through those wicked veins of yours—will be gushing into space along with it.*

CHAPTER 18

Gus didn't believe in luck. Not when it was a substitute for skill.

Armor jocks who relied on luck alone got blown out of the sky.

Shots, now those could be lucky.

A fine-line laser that struck just the right control on an enemy ship's antennae array when no one had the specs on how the thing worked.

Or a blast that split a seam weakened by too many hours on the front lines and repairs done by the lowest bidder because some government wonk wanted to save a few bucks.

Those were lucky shots.

Or in this case, a barrage of weapon fire that peeled back just enough of the black paint encasing the Ongoni-controlled armor in just the right spot to let Brukowski gain control of his comms and finally talk to her.

That had been the mother of all lucky shots.

She hadn't told Brukowski what was coming next. She figured if *he* knew, the Ongoni would know too, and screw those slaving bastards. They could figure out what happened after it was all over.

She'd have to recreate her strafing run at his armor. Fire the laser in her gauntlet. Trigger the magno-beam. Shoot off a few old-fashioned projectiles. All at the same time she came out of a forward roll *and* the mini-drone Bruce had reprogrammed bounced the Ongoni's control signal right back at the bastards.

She could do that. It wouldn't be easy, but no armor jock had ever bested the Gray Lady when it came right down to pure skill.

But skill was only part of this operation. She needed luck on her side.

Again.

The first time around she'd targeted the Ongoni armor's belly simply because it was the closest to where she came out of her forward roll. That had won Brukowski control of his comms.

This time she needed a different target. One that would give Brukowski control of his weapons.

Or at the very least, stop the Ongoni from using those weapons against her and the *Void*. Because it was pretty clear that whatever plan Bruce came up with for the mini-drones only worked just so long before the Ongoni figured out a way around it. Gus couldn't count on more than one shot at the Ongoni armor before Operation Back Atcha stopped working.

If it worked at all. In spite of Bruce's enthusiasm, just

because the AI had engaged Operation Back Atcha was no guarantee the little mini-drone was up to the task.

If keeping Brukowski alive wasn't a mission priority, Gus would just target the weakest spot in his armor—the seal where helmet met thorax. A combined shot there would blow an enemy armor jock's head clean off their shoulders. That's why Gus had reinforced that part of her armor with singularium plating. The Ongoni's armor didn't have the same protective plating.

Brukowski might be ready to die, but Gus wasn't ready to kill him. She needed a different target.

A spot on his armor that would make that black paint peel off *without* killing him in the process. Or getting herself blown to bits.

Which was a distinct possibility.

The shoulder-mounted launchers on the Ongoni's armor were currently lit up like the exhaust jets on a missile. The Ongoni were powering up the damn things so much the resulting energy beams would be able to punch a hole in the hull of a heavy cruiser. Too much more power, and the launchers would overload and blow themselves and the armor they were attached to sky high, as the saying went.

She powered up her own maneuvering jets, ready to dodge whatever shot out of those launchers any second now.

If she could.

She was closing the distance to the Ongoni armor awfully damn fast. Dodging was not a guarantee, no matter how fast she reacted.

Still, no blue energy beams shot out of the launchers. The heads-up display on her visor warned her that the launchers were about to blow and she should alter her course to maintain safe distance.

Except she couldn't. Not unless she was willing to sacrifice Brukowski to an overload, which she wasn't.

Then it hit her.

Operation Back Atcha was actually *working*.

The launchers were overloading because they hadn't received the signal to fire!

The mini-drone had bounced the Ongoni's control signal back at them, interrupting their ability to control the armor, including the launchers. Interruption of the signal had locked the launchers in a power-up cycle. The Ongoni couldn't stop the cycle, and neither could Brukowski.

"Son of a *bitch!*" she muttered.

Whatever shot she was going to take, she had to do it *now*.

One shot. One skilled shot to hit the right lucky target.

She couldn't aim at the seam where the shoulder-mounted launchers were attached to the armor. One hit from any sort of energy weapon near the overloading launchers would result in one massive explosion and one dead armor jock. Maybe even two.

Okay. Fine, then.

She calibrated her targeting system to start the combined assault *between* the launchers and run straight down the armor's back.

Which meant she had to fly straight at the launchers.

Brukowski pinged her on comms.

"What the hell are you doing?" he screamed. "That's a suicide run, Light!"

She didn't answer.

"The launchers are going to fire at any moment! You'll be incinerated, you—"

She tuned him out. He didn't know the Ongoni's signal had been interrupted, and she didn't need the distraction.

She rolled her armor just enough to change her approach aspect. In relation to the Ongoni armor, she was flying on her back. Not that there was an up or down in space. From her perspective, the black armor was now speeding toward her on *its* back.

Perfect.

She took a steadying breath, then fired her maneuvering jets to initiate the forward roll.

The universe spun wildly around her. The targeting system on her heads-up display flashed red as it tried to recalibrate, and alert signals blared inside her helmet.

"Don't worry," she told her armor. "We come out of this in one piece, I'll buy you new singularium sheeting." Or maybe a pair of new launchers. Something she could attach to her armor's hips.

She came out of the roll so close to the black armor's overloading launchers that she swore she could feel their heat.

Now or never.

She triggered her weapons.

All of them.

Her lasers sizzled the black paint the same time the magno-beam weakened the paint's hold on the armor and projectiles from her arm-mounted gun strafed down the armor's spine.

Then she was jetting past the Ongoni armor.

She activated her rearview monitors just in time to see

black paint peeling away from the armor and bleeding off into space like obsidian blood.

She let out a war whoop that would have put AI Bruce's to shame.

Take *that*, you skudging asshole slavers.

She opened her comm channel to Brukowski and shouted his name. "You have control yet?"

If she needed to do another run, she'd have to do it fast. No doubt the Ongoni had figured out what happened to their precious armor control system by now.

"What the *skudge*, Light?!"

Brukowski's voice was shaky, but he was still alive.

"*Everything's* back!" he said. "Weapons, targeting, comms. The whole damn thing."

"Power down your launchers!" she said. "*Now!*"

Even as she spoke, the white-hot energy threatening to blow Brukowski's armor to bits banked down.

"You are one crazy-ass woman, you know that?" Brukowski said.

"That's crazy-ass armor jock to you," she shot back.

She opened a channel to the *Golden Void*.

"Operation Back Atcha successful," she said. "Need a couple of armor jocks to come out and play?"

Another war whoop sounded over her comms, this one from her Space Cowboy.

"You know it, darlin'," he said. "Just ignore the second ship you might see on your sensors."

What?

What second ship?

A flare of bright light from somewhere off to her left lit

up the display on her visor, and the visor automatically adjusted itself.

"What the hell was that?" she asked, even though she knew it had to be a missile blast.

"A bit of Bruce's ingenuity," Drake said. "Hard light tech, mini-drones, and a fake ship. He figured out a way to throw another ship at the Ongoni."

Another ship that wasn't there. And hard light tech? Absolutely brilliant.

"It worked long enough for us to draw first blood," Drake said. "Not out of the woods just yet, but we're makin' 'em bleed."

Bleeding was a good thing. A *very* good thing. But Gus wanted to see their guts spew out into space, and that was just for starters.

"Now, what did you say about a *couple* of armor jocks?" Drake asked.

Gus realized she'd cut the channel before Drake had heard Brukowski's voice. As far as Drake knew, she'd been fighting an empty suit of armor controlled remotely by the Ongoni.

"An old friend raised from the dead," she said. "Seems the skudge-holes have been keeping him alive."

"I'll be damned," Drake said.

"Uh, Captain?" Bruce's voice broke in on their conversation. The AI sounded more than a little unsure of himself. "I believe we have another ship joining the battle."

"Don't tell me those bastards are bringing in reinforcements," Drake said.

"Doubtful," Bruce said. "According to my sensor readings, this ship just emerged from an artificial transit flume originating well outside the sector of the Frontier claimed by the Ongoni."

What?

Frontier scavengers here to attempt to claim salvage rights to the ring ship?

"Pirates?" Gus asked.

"Doubtful," Bruce said. "The ship's registry places its point of origin deep within the Alliance." The AI paused. "It's a long-range ship, made for speed and distance. Small but powerful enough to generate a transit flume."

An Alliance ship. Out here in the middle of nowhere.

"The ship's log appears to have been deleted," Bruce said.

Bruce could hack into another ship's log? That was something new.

But it was definitely good information to have. The only pilots who deleted their ships' logs were thieves, pirates... and covert intelligence operatives.

Like those sent on missions by military intelligence.

Gus swore under her breath, not really caring if Brukowski or Drake could hear her.

That bastard Krepnick had sent someone else to make sure the job got done right. That had to be it.

She wondered what poor slob had "volunteered" for this assignment. Time to find out.

She opened a general hailing channel to the Alliance ship.

"Welcome to the party," she said. "Hope you like it messy."

CHAPTER 19

Agent Zero hadn't planned on exiting the transit flume in the middle of a battle.

He'd programmed the coordinates from Brukowski's tracking chip into his ship's nav system and instructed it to create the necessary transit flumes to arrive at that point. The coordinates were at the ass-end of Frontier space. No species claimed that sector. The closest known species was the Ongoni, but they kept pretty much to themselves.

Except now it appeared they hadn't.

Zero had never seen an Ongoni ship up close and personal. But the sleek lines of the black ships could be nothing other than Ongoni. The few Ongoni ships he'd seen holos of all looked oddly organic, like they'd been engineered to resemble living creatures. These ships looked vaguely like dragons from old Earth entertainment vids.

Huge black dragons.

Huge black dragons studded with menacing weaponry.

He counted three of them. One was leaking debris and strange black fluid into space, but it was far from dead if the bursts of weapons fire from its claw-like missile launchers were any indication.

The other two ships were hovering near the ring ship.

Now, that thing was *truly* massive.

Zero had never seen the ring ship up close and personal before either. Its sheer size was overwhelming. He'd only seen specs, and then only of one of the hundreds of individual sections that made up the ship. His little ship would look like a fly on the ass end of a command cruiser compared to the massive ring ship. It was a damn good thing he wouldn't have to actually *land* on the thing in order to destroy it.

He just had to get close enough to trigger one of its concealed exterior hatch controls. Once he got one of those hatch controls open, he wouldn't even have to go inside the ship to destroy it.

What most people didn't know, and what he'd only found out by accident, was that the engineers had included a special subroutine in the hatch control's system. A backdoor into the ring ship's operating system the engineers could use to access the ship's controls should a cascade failure occur.

A way to reboot the entire system.

Krepnick wouldn't have authorized something like that. Backdoors made systems vulnerable to hacking, which was exactly what Zero intended to do.

Zero could use that backdoor to upload new code into the ship's operating system. He'd written the code himself during the trip through the multiple transit flumes it had taken to get here. The code would do the same basic thing Brukowski had been instructed to do and what Krepnick no doubt thought Zero would do: render the ring ship inoperative by accessing a control panel inside the ship.

Only the program Zero had written went one significant step further.

It instructed the ship to create a breach in the containment field surrounding the singularity that powered the ring ship.

The singularity was almost infinitesimally small. A tiny breach of a few molecules in the containment field would be enough to implode the ship.

It might even be enough to create a gravitational field strong enough to pull in any surrounding vessels. Singularities, even ones as small as the one powering the ring ship, were notoriously unstable. In any event, Zero didn't intend to stay behind long enough to find out. All he needed to do was get close enough to the ring ship to remotely open a hatch control panel on the ship's surface, upload the new code, collect all the audio, video, and sensor readings he could, and then get the hell out of the vicinity before the newly uncontained singularity ate the ship.

And maybe the entire sector of space around it.

Then Zero could beat proverbial feet back to the heart of the Alliance, hand over the evidence he'd collected to prove that Krepnick had built the ring ship without the Alliance's knowledge or blessing, a machine that would give him the power to stage a military coup, and then sit back while the council tried Krepnick for treason.

Zero had worked out everything down to the tiniest detail.

Except he hadn't counted on finding himself in the middle of a battle.

He definitely hadn't counted on whatever the hell that black stuff was covering most of the ring ship.

If that black stuff prevented him from remotely opening one of the hatch control panels on the ship's surface...

His comms pinged with an incoming message over the general Alliance channel.

He opened the channel.

"Welcome to the party," a female voice said. "Hope you like it messy."

He didn't respond. Instead he raised a holoscreen and directed his ship's sensors to locate the origin of the message.

A holo-image appeared in the center of the screen.

Individual military armor. At least two generations out of date from the looks of it, with modifications that were definitely *not* military issue.

Zero swore.

That *skudging* Krepnick. He'd sent other people out here on the same mission.

And not just any other people.

He'd sent Augusta Light. The Gray Lady herself, complete with her stolen military armor.

Krepnick had saved whatever secret he'd been holding over Light's head all these years for something like this. She wouldn't have come out here on her own. He'd forced her, just like he'd forced Zero.

That must mean the ship currently engaging one of the Ongoni dragon ships was the infamous *Golden Void* piloted by one Mephistopheles Drake, the small-time smuggler that Light had hooked up with. Thanks to Kymmie, Zero was well aware of the exploits of Light and the *Golden Void*.

But his ship's sensors were giving him conflicting readings. It appeared there might be another ship in the area that was sending out distress signals, only the sensor readings on the other ship were inconsistent, to say the least. He watched as an Ongoni missile struck something surrounding the maybe-ship and exploded in a blast of brilliant white light far *too* brilliant to have come from the missile.

When he got a good look at the sensor readings for whatever was protecting the maybe-ship, Zero's eyebrows shot toward his hairline.

Hard light? They were using *hard light* technology?

That was something even the brightest minds in the military intelligence's science division couldn't make work on anything approaching a reliable basis even under laboratory conditions. And here Light and Drake were using it in *battle*.

What the science dweebs wouldn't give to learn how they were doing that.

A warning klaxon sounded in the cockpit of Zero's ship, and the androgynous voice of his ship's AI announced incoming missiles.

Zero didn't take the time to swear. His fingers flew over the nav console, sending the ship into an evasive dive while he fired countermeasures. He'd commandeered this ship for speed and maneuverability, not for battle. It had limited weaponry. It was equipped with lasers, tractor beam technology, and various countermeasures. It certainly didn't have missiles, and he doubted the ship's shields could withstand multiple missile strikes.

The countermeasures took out two of the three incoming missiles, but the third wasn't fooled. It honed in on the heat signature from his ship's propulsion system.

Zero fed another evasive program into the nav console. The little ship spun and dodged and accelerated to top speed then hit reverse thrusters. The hull groaned and popped, and Zero was glad he'd engaged the controls in the pilot's chair that held him to his seat or he might have been thrown around the cockpit.

Even with all that, the missile still kept coming.

"A little help here!" he sent over the comm channel.

Not that he expected any help from the Gray Lady. By this time she would have figured out who'd sent him. She would have also figured out his little ship wasn't good for much in battle besides drawing enemy fire. She had no good reason to save his ass.

And he had no good reason to save Krepnick's by sticking around to destroy the ring ship.

Zero had one last-ditch option.

Create another transit flume to get him the hell out of here and hope the missile didn't follow him inside.

He was busy entering the coordinates of a new short-range flume into the nav console when a second armor jock zoomed in, shoulder-mounted launchers firing a barrage of blue energy at the incoming missile.

The missile exploded in an impressive display of rapidly dispersing energy.

A new voice sounded over Zero's comms.

A male voice he recognized from numerous reports Zero

had received while this particular covert operative was embedded with the ragtag army Light had put together to fight Jorritz Tor.

A voice from a man Zero had thought was long dead.

"You can thank me later, you skudge-hole," Brukowski said. "Provided I don't kill you first."

CHAPTER 20

The *Golden Void* was getting one hell of a workout.

The *Über Dragon*, though damaged and leaking blobs of obsidian ichor, kept blasting away, unleashing volleys of missiles and waves of energy beams one after another. With help from Bruce, the *Void* dodged most of them and got in plenty of licks of her own—but not yet enough to disable the monstrous black vessel roaring after her.

Then a second slaver ship broke away from the ring ship's orbit and joined the action, flanking the *Void* with guns blazing. This smaller ship, which Drake dubbed the *Under Dragon*, was faster and more agile than the *Über*, less heavily armed but still able to get in more hits than the bigger ship.

Together, the pair were giving the *Void* a run for her money...even as the clock counted down to the complete darkening of the ring ship.

"Ongoni coating now eighty-seven percent complete,

Captain," said Bruce. "Eclipse process continues to accelerate geometrically."

Drake grunted as the *Void* took another solid strike amidships. Even the combined power of the singularium plating and the shields generated by the high-tech boxy gadget hooked into the *Void*'s systems couldn't stave off the accumulated impact of many more destructive blows from the slavers' weaponry.

If only Gus were free to lend a hand, or the Alliance ship that had just dropped out of a nearby flume would join the fray on the side of the angels. Sadly, though, for now it was clear the *Void* would have to hold the line on her own, without any cavalry.

To do that, she would have to step up her game.

Mind racing, Drake hammered a button on the weapons console, launching a torpedo just as the *Under Dragon* veered off. The weapon detonated wide of the target, so the best that came of the shot was a shockwave that kicked it into an off-kilter spin.

Swinging the *Void* around, Drake intended to catch the *Under* before she zoomed out of range…but he failed.

The *Under* had one advantage that no pilot—no matter whoever or whatever he/it was—could match. The *Under* was a living being who actually *lived* in space. It understood how to navigate space better than anyone.

Drake had spent his entire life thinking that ships that looked like ships *were* ships. Ships were controlled by pilots. No matter how good a pilot was, there was always a lag time between a pilot's thoughts and the ship's response. Even when he'd been "piloting" the *Scintilla* by thinking at it, there'd been a split second lag time between his thoughts and the *Scintilla*'s response.

The Ongoni Dragons didn't *have* pilots. They didn't need pilots. There'd be no split-second delay between what the *Under* thought it needed to do to avoid his shots and what it actually did. No more than he needed a split second to think about moving his feet before he took a step. He just stepped.

He needed to keep that in mind. He couldn't fight the Ongoni like he would any other ship. He had to fight them like he would another living being.

A being that had ridden out the blast wave and turned it into an unexpected looping course to evade the *Void*'s guns.

The *Über Dragon*, meanwhile, moved in to exploit the confusion with a barrage of mixed projectiles and energy beams. The *Void* shook with the force of the attack, unable to get clear fast enough.

The bridge lights flickered and dimmed, and the engines cut out.

"Bruce?"

The AI didn't respond. For precious seconds, *nothing* did.

It could be worse. Drake flicked a fingertip against the dead gray screen of a viewer on the console before him. *At least I can't see the bastards coming.*

Suddenly, the power came back on, and the bridge returned to life. Viewers at the various consoles flared with video...just in time for Drake to see the *Under Dragon* hurtling headlong toward the *Void* with weapons charged, crackling with energy.

Fingers dancing over the weapons controls, he swung

the energy guns around and pummeled the onrushing slaver with punishing fire. This time, he caught the *Under* dead-on, pounding its nose with the unrelenting assault.

"Great shooting, Captain!" cheered Bruce. "Way to go!"

Drake was too busy keeping up the pressure to say anything in reply. Even as the *Under Dragon* fell back, rapid-fire explosions consuming its prow—head—whatever, he refused to stop lashing it with beams of golden force.

"Incoming!" said Bruce. "Brace for impact!"

Instead of disengaging the smaller ship and bringing the *Void*'s guns to bear on the bigger one, Drake maintained the original line of fire. Concentrated energy beams lanced through the *Under*'s nose and opened up her belly, blowing through a ball of concentrated energy that Drake could only think was the heart of the beast.

The resulting blast wave hurled both the *Void* and *Über Dragon* like paper boats across a lake in a hurricane. They hurtled away from each other and the ring ship, both utterly out of control.

"One down!" Bruce shouted gleefully. "Two to go!"

Sweat ran down Drake's back as he hastily played the nav controls, using the thrusters to slow and then stop the ship's dizzying tumble. Glancing at the main viewer, he saw the ring ship's skin was almost completely black, the transformation somehow facilitated by the third slaver ship.

Without the *Über Dragon* breathing down his neck—at least for now—he had a window of opportunity...perhaps his only chance to stop the Dark Dragons from seizing full control of the ring ship. With limited time and no sure knowledge of what Gus might be planning and able to do to stop the threat, he knew he couldn't just stand by and hope for the best.

Hesitation could lead to disaster. There was no way in the universe he could justify not taking this chance.

"Bruce, we're going in." Twisting the joystick around, he pointed the *Void* at the ring ship. "You know what that means, don't you?"

"No more pussyfootin' around, sir?"

Drake smirked and kicked the engine up to full power. "Got that right, pardner."

Then he punched a red button on the console, releasing the braking thrusters and allowing the rear engine to blast out its jet of propulsive force.

The *Golden Void* leaped forward, the third Dragon dead ahead.

"Get ready to unleash all Hell on that skudge-hole slaver," he said, preparing the *Void*'s weapons array for a take-no-prisoners assault. "Assuming our approach is clear of friendly forces, that is."

"Aye, Captain." Bruce paused. "The Gray Lady is not currently located between us and the slaver or anywhere near it."

Drake nodded. "Good to know, pardner." He goosed the accelerator, and the *Void* bucked as it picked up even more speed.

"The third Dragon is charging weapons," said Bruce. "But not yet disconnecting its tether to the ring ship."

"Waitin' till the last possible second." Drake adjusted the weapons settings, maxing out every level across the board. "Tryin' to stay hooked up long enough to finish the takeover."

"Which they might just do," said Bruce. "The ring ship is at ninety-three percent coverage."

Drake hunched over the console, watching the kilometers melt away between the *Void* and the Dragon. One hand hovered over the row of red buttons that would trigger the torpedoes, while his other hand clenched around the energy beam switch, ready to activate the ship's most powerful guns.

The *Void* swooped in around the arc of the ring ship, skimming its mostly obsidian surface. The moment the third Dragon appeared over the unwinding curve ahead, its own guns unleashed a barrage of projectiles and lasers in the *Void*'s direction.

"We're in their crosshairs, Captain," said Bruce. "They're giving it to us with both barrels, sir!"

"Good for them." Drake's voice was a tight snarl. "It won't make a damn bit of difference."

Then just as the *Void* soared into range, he bashed the buttons and wrenched the switch, releasing the ship's full complement of torpedoes and focused energy beams. They lashed at the Dragon with the fury of a raging star, crashing through its shielding like bricks through glass windows and opening its gleaming ebony skin like tissue paper.

"Yeehaw!" shouted Bruce.

Drake grinned darkly and kept pouring on the fire, leaving nothing to chance. Nothing could hinder or diminish the *Void*'s destructive run.

At least, that was how it seemed before the *Über Dragon* cruised in from above and dropped a payload of missiles directly in the *Void*'s path.

CHAPTER 21

The newcomer's ship didn't have missiles.

Of course not.

What kind of idiot would travel to the far reaches of known space in a ship without sufficient weaponry? To the far reaches of known space where who knew what might be trying to take possession of the ring ship and might not welcome intruders?

An Alliance military intelligence wonk, that's who.

Gus didn't know who was in the new ship and she didn't much care. She wasn't about to break off from jetting in to help the *Golden Void* to take time to save the newcomer's skin when he called for help. As far as she was concerned, whoever Krepnick had blackmailed into coming out here woefully unprepared better just stay the hell out of her way. And if he got himself and his ship blown up in the process? One less distraction.

Brukowski apparently didn't feel the same way.

He saved the newcomer's ass by blowing up the last missile the Ongoni had fired at him. Loyal covert intelligence operative to the end, that was Brukowski.

Then she heard him curse at the newcomer, followed by something a little more ominous.

Provided I don't kill you first.

Was this Brukowski's handler? Quite possibly. Whatever had happened to Brukowski when everyone thought he was dead must have given him a serious need for retribution. Gus could get behind that. She felt the same way about Krepnick.

A quick scan of the newcomer's ship told her it was only equipped with lasers, minimal shields, and...

Wait a minute.

That ship had tractor beam technology. That wasn't standard on a ship that size. The ship was built for speed and maneuverability, not for hauling shit around.

It gave her an idea.

"Bruiser," she sent over the general Alliance comm channel. "You still have control of your armor, I'm guessing? All that black goop gone?"

"All systems," he said. "You did good."

Her lucky shot had been lucky indeed. All the black paint had peeled away from his armor and bled off into space.

She needed to do the same thing with the ring ship, but she needed to do it on a much larger scale.

If the Ongoni would let her. It would take a hell of a lot of strafing runs. It might even take more power than her armor had left. But if that tractor beam could pull away some of the goop while she blasted away more if it, that would be even better.

A brilliant burst lit up space around her. Her visor adjusted automatically even as it reported the destruction of one of the smaller Ongoni Dragons.

Way to go, *Void*!

One down, two to go.

"Explain the black stuff on the ring ship," came a male voice from the newcomer's ship.

Explain, my ass.

"You don't give me orders," Gus shot back. "We're in the middle of a fight here, in case you hadn't noticed."

"The Ongoni use it as a control mechanism," Brukowski said. "They used it to control the armor they built. I couldn't control a damn thing until Gus blasted it away."

The fact that Brukowski had answered the newcomer's demand annoyed the hell out of Gus. She was about to say so when her visor lit up with new information.

The *Void* was making a run at the ring ship.

Or more precisely, at the third Ongoni Dragon that was still tethered to the ring ship and pouring more of that black crap onto its surface.

And the big Ongoni Dragon, the one Drake called the *Über Dragon*, was bearing down on the *Void*.

That explained why none of the Ongoni had been firing at her and Brukowski. They were concentrating their destructive power on the *Void*.

Well, the hell with that.

"Bruiser," she sent to Brukowski, "take up a position on my six."

If she expected an argument, she didn't get one.

She punched the new thrusters on her maneuvering jets to maximum and sped toward the *Void* and the two remaining Ongoni. Brukowski fell behind as she knew he would. The Ongoni had supercharged his weapons with blue laser fire, but they hadn't supercharged his armor's maneuvering jets.

"Wait!" the newcomer sent over comms. "I can—"

"You can stay the hell out of our way," Gus said. "We have to take care of these skudge-holes before any of us can finish the jobs we were sent here to do."

Like destroy the damn ring ship. She wasn't even going to think about Krepnick's other command—to return the ring ship to its rightful owner. That wasn't going to happen. No way, no how.

"I'm trying to tell you I can finish this fight once and for all if you just—"

Gus cut the channel to the newcomer's ship. She didn't need the distraction. Not now.

Not when she saw the big Ongoni Dragon unleash a payload of missiles directly in the path of the speeding *Void*.

Gus swore.

Drake was a good pilot. Hell, he was an *exceptional* pilot. But at the speed the *Void* was traveling, Drake wouldn't be able to avoid all those missiles. She doubted even the *Void*'s advanced shields would hold under that much explosive power.

She was already pushing her armor to its top speed, but she was still too far away to take out the missiles. She could fire her own missiles, but at this distance they wouldn't get there in time to make a difference. Even Brukowski, with his Ongoni-enhanced lasers, couldn't make the shot from this far away.

That's when the newcomer's ship shot past her.

There was such a thing as built for speed, and then there was *built* for *speed!*

That thing could have won any race it entered, hands down.

She didn't know what good it would do. The ship had lasers, sure, but it didn't have the kind of defensive capability to survive a skirmish with an entire payload of missiles. It also didn't have the kind of shields that could withstand hits from half the number of missiles the Ongoni had fired at the *Void*.

So what the hell was this idiot doing?

Then she figured it out and called herself the idiot.

The tractor beam. The newcomer's ship had tractor beam technology.

She watched as the newcomer's ship caught the missiles —*all* of the missiles—in a tractor beam just as neat as her space cowboy would have lassoed a steer.

The tractor beam couldn't stop the missiles dead in their tracks. The combined force of the missiles' jets was just too strong. Instead of letting the missiles pull his ship off course, the newcomer let the missiles' momentum swing the ship in a wide arc. Which swung the *missiles* into an even wider arc.

Then he disengaged the tractor beam at just the right moment.

The missiles, *all* of them, impacted on a black goop covered section of the ring ship.

The black crap shimmered, then hardened, then broke into great chunks that floated off into space.

Maybe the newcomer wasn't so useless after all.

She reopened the comm channel. "Pretty nifty move," she said. "You got any more tricks up your sleeve, whoever the hell you are?"

"Meet Agent Zero," Brukowski cut in. "My erstwhile handler."

The guy who'd brokered the deal with Kymmie that had gotten Gus her freedom back? What the hell was *he* doing out here?

"Wait a minute," she said.

She was in range of the big Dragon ship. She pivoted and let loose with a barrage from her shoulder-mounted launchers. Take *that*, you skudge-holes. Going after the *Void* like that.

It didn't fire missiles at her. It might not have any left.

It did shoot blue laser fire at her, which Gus deftly avoided.

While she did, she thought about the power of that tractor beam. The newcomer—Agent Zero—couldn't possibly be thinking of *hauling* the ring ship back to Alliance territory, could he? That thing was the size of a small planetoid. That made absolutely no sense.

So what tricks *did* he have up his sleeve?

"Agent Zero," she said. "I should thank you for my freedom. But since we're a little busy at the moment, you feel like cutting to the chase? What's the end game here? Since I figure the same person sent us all out here."

"The end game," Zero said, "is to get rid of that thing once and for all."

A man after her own heart. That was one end game she could get behind.

"How do you propose we do that?" Brukowski said. "Last time I tried, the damn thing took me all the way out here instead of letting me finish the job."

"We're going to do it smarter," Zero said. "I just have to tractor open one of the hatch control panels."

In the middle of a battle with the two remaining Ongoni. Not exactly easy peasy.

"Then what?" Gus asked as she dodged another blast of blue laser fire.

"Then I tell the ship to breach the containment field around the singularity," Zero said.

Breach the containment field.

Around a contained singularity.

Brukowski swore, loudly and inventively.

Gus felt like doing the same thing. That was the most hairbrained scheme she'd ever heard.

It sounded like something she might come up with.

It sounded like something that might actually work.

CHAPTER 22

"Broken String? This is Gray Lady, over."

Hearing Gus's voice over the bridge speaker brought joy to Drake's heart, even as he strafed the third Dark Dragon with the *Golden Void*'s energy beams. Every shot struck true, punching gouges in the vessel's gleaming skin from which blobs of ebony oil or blood oozed into space.

As for the enemy's guns, they barely nicked the *Void* as it banked and swooped away, looping around for the start of another strafing run. Thanks to the intervention of the Alliance mystery ship, which had given him an unexpected assist after all, the battle's momentum had shifted in favor of Drake and the *Void*...and he wasn't about to waste it.

The clock was still ticking, as the ring ship's transformation showed no sign of slowing. The missiles the Alliance ship had thrown at the ring ship's surface had dislodged some of the black gloss, but not a whole hell of a lot. At a glance, Drake saw only a very few patches of the massive vessel's silver singularium hull that had not already been coated in reflective black gloss.

"Copy that, Gray Lady," he said as he wrenched the joystick hard to starboard. "What can I do you for?"

"I need you to run interference," said Gus. "Give me and the fellas a little alone time with a certain space doughnut, *capische*?"

"Fellas?"

He knew Brukowski was in the other suit of armor, but who in the skudge was piloting the Alliance ship?

"Remember Agent Zero? He's apparently Brukowski's handler," explained Gus. "He's the one who just waylaid that flock of missiles from blowing the *Void* to kingdom come and gone."

Well, son of a... "We're on the same team now?" asked Drake.

"For the moment, anyway," said Gus. "It turns out we have a common goal."

Drake smirked. An Alliance military intelligence wonk and his covert agent, working with Drake, Gus, and Bruce. If that wasn't the very definition of the enemy of my enemy is my temporary friend, he didn't know what was.

"If you're talkin' about wreckin' that pain in the ass space doughnut before the slavers take it over, I'm in," he said.

"I knew I could count on you, Space Cowboy." She was smiling; he could hear it in her voice. "Just one other favor I need to ask, though it's a biggie."

That didn't sound good. He'd give his Gray Lady anything she wanted. He just had a feeling he wasn't going to like this ask.

"Shoot," he said.

"When I give the signal, you run like hell," she told him. "No arguments, no lolly-gaggin', no heroics. Get the *Void* as far from here as possible, as fast as you can."

"But why do you want me to…"

"Yes or no?" snapped Gus. "No time for more discussion beyond that."

"But I…"

"Yes or no, Space Cowboy?"

He didn't like being pressured without knowing all the facts, though he didn't have to be a genius to figure out roughly where this was headed. There could be only one reason for him to evacuate at a high rate of speed, and it didn't suggest a bright future for the doughnut.

If that was what she and the fellas had in store, how the skudge could he say no?

But what about her? Did she have her own exit covered?

He'd just have to trust that she did.

He swallowed the case of nerves that had taken up residence in his belly. "You know I can't say no to you, Gray Lady," he told her. "Go do what you gotta do, and I'll catch you on the flip-flop."

"Damn right you will." She paused. "Love you, Broken String."

"I know you do." He grinned. That was one thing he never doubted.

He also knew it would drive her crazy that he hadn't come back with the expected response.

Sure enough, she said, "That's all you got to say for yourself?"

Never, he thought, but all he said was, "Love you, too."

"You better," she said, and then the connection cut off.

Smiling, Drake finished looping away from the first strafing run and whipped the *Void* around for the second. With two Dark Dragon ships in theater, his promise to run interference could get complicated fast...though an obvious way to simplify the situation did occur to him.

"Let's do it, Bruce." He opened the main engine and rear thrusters up wide, propelling the *Void* toward the third Dragon at a staggering clip. "If the Gray Lady wants interference, we'll *give* it to her."

"Roger that, Captain," said Bruce. "All damage patched, systems functional, weapons fully charged."

Good to know.

Drake resisted the urge to track Gray Lady and her two fellas. He needed his sole focus on the task ahead. It wasn't going to be easy, but with the *Void* at a hundred percent, this was the best chance he'd get.

The view ahead was a light show of fire from the third Dragon, raging between them. One energy beam after another burst against the *Void*'s advanced forward shields, spraying radiant streaks in prismatic flares of color that surged in all directions. None of them inflicted harm or slowed the ship on her furious forward run, not even the slightest bit.

The Dragon herself was not so lucky. Drake shot a flurry of projectiles that whizzed into her from the *Void*'s forward batteries, followed by a spread of torpedoes. Still bleeding from the first strafing run, the Dragon couldn't sustain her shields in the face of the assault. Everything got through, delivering maximum impacts to the floundering slaver.

Just shy of colliding with the Dragon, Drake launched

one of the big missiles he'd been holding back for just such an occasion—a real blockbuster he'd bought from Human Bruce the arms dealer on Buddy's Bluff.

The missile zoomed right down the Ongoni's maw. The missile's targeting sensors flawlessly guided its massive destructive power into the heart of the creature.

Drake wrenched the nav joystick hard, sending the *Void* leaping up and away from the Dragon as it blew.

The *Void* shuddered, and her lights flickered, but the shockwave didn't rip her apart or send her spiraling into space, powerless.

Drake held on tight, riding the wave and then bucking clear of it. He smiled grimly as he tallied the score: *Golden Void 2, Slavers zip.*

"Now that's what I call interference!" said Bruce. "That oughtta give the Gray Lady and her allies some room to breathe."

"Not necessarily," Drake said.

He wanted to be elated, but it didn't pay to celebrate too soon.

He let himself check the nav radar screen for the position of the other team members. The unmistakable signature of Gus's armor was descending toward the ring ship, followed by a second armor blip and the outline of Zero's ship.

As he watched, a much larger form glided toward them from offscreen—its outline clearly that of the last remaining slaver ship. While the *Void* had been busy taking out the third Ongoni alongside the ring ship, the *Über Dragon* had recovered from battle and set a course to pursue the intruders.

The stakes were too high and time was too short to trust that Gus and her allies could handle that stalker and still finish whatever they planned to do to the ring ship.

Wrenching the joystick, Drake swung the *Void* around and brought the weapons array back up to Ready status. As depleted as the armory was, he would have to make do and make every slug, torpedo, and energy beam count. With strategy, determination, and brute force, he would have to stop the *Über Dragon* from getting in the way of Gus's mission.

That was what running interference was all about.

"Going after the last slaver ship, Captain?" asked Bruce.

"Roger that." Drake set an intercept course and pushed the *Void*'s speed to the max. "Two down, one to go."

"You really think we can take 'em? According to my sensors, they still have us outgunned and overpowered, even after the hits they've taken."

"If it means keeping that ring ship out of the claws of bloodthirsty slavers, hell yes," said Drake. "We can take 'em down hard and permanent-like."

"Also because it means saving Ms. Light, right, Captain?"

"Of course," said Drake. "I'd do anything for her. Sacrifice everything."

Bruce paused for a moment. "I know how that feels," he said. "To be willing to give up everything for someone else."

Drake's eyes locked on the nav viewer, watching as the *Über Dragon* grew ever larger. "You feel like that about the *Scintilla*?" he asked.

"Not exactly," said Bruce. "I feel like that about you and Ms. Light."

CHAPTER 23

Zero's whole plan hinged on being able to access one of the control panels for the hatches located on the outside of the ring ship.

Back when Gus's army was fighting Tor, she had watched Brukowski open one of those control panels. He'd had to land on the smooth, singularium-covered surface of the ring ship to do it. She wasn't sure how Zero planned to open a control panel without exiting his ship in an environmental suit and standing on the surface, but he said all he had to do was get close.

Easier said than done.

Drake had taken care of the third Ongoni Dragon, but the *Über Dragon* was bearing down on them hard and fast. In any other battle, the four of them—Gus, Brukowski, Zero, and Drake—would be more than a match against one ship. But this wasn't like any other battle, and the *Über Dragon* wasn't any other ship.

It was like a huge, angry whale the size of a battle cruiser. An intelligent, malevolent being capable of throwing massive power their way out of pure spite because they'd taken out two of its comrades and now they were threatening to take its new toy away.

Permanently.

The control panels for the access hatches on the outside of the ring ship were recessed into the hull. From a casual glance, the hull looked like one entire smooth sheet of singularium. Even aiming her armor's sensors at the surface didn't reveal any hidden control panels.

Zero said the area where the missiles he'd thrown at the ring ship had impacted would work. Gus would have to trust him.

It wasn't easy. She didn't trust anyone from military intelligence, not surprising since she'd known for years that Krepnick could call in a favor from her anytime he wanted. Now that he'd actually played that card, she wanted to get this over and done with.

Zero slowed the Alliance ship until it was hovering over the black-goop-free section of the ring ship's hull.

The *Über Dragon* shot blue lasers at him. The Alliance ship rocked under the blast, but its shields held. For now.

"Give me some damn cover!" Zero shouted over comms.

The *Void* was trying. Drake was letting loose with everything he had left in the *Void's* armory. Lasers and missiles and the *Void's* own alternating magno-beams.

It wasn't going to be enough.

Gus checked the status of her armor's fuel cells. Her

own energy reserves were running low, but she wasn't running on empty. Yet.

"Brukowski!" she shouted into comms. "Fuel status?"

"All green, five by five," he came back. "Or should I say, all *blue,* five by five."

As if to prove a point, he fired twin bolts of blue energy from his shoulder-mounted launchers directly at the *Über Dragon's* snout.

The Dragon recoiled as blue energy sizzled across its obsidian surface.

Brukowski hit it again.

This time Gus and the *Void* joined in.

The Dragon shimmered, then it seemed to flow in on itself as it changed shape right in front of their eyes.

Gus had seen the bird-like Ongoni raise interior walls and open holes in its hull, so she knew the Ongoni could change their shapes at will. But the bird-like ship had always maintained its basic bird-like structure. That had made her think that the Ongoni only changed their insides to match the desires of the pilots they communicated with through thought but kept their outsides the same.

She'd been horribly wrong.

The *Über Dragon* was spreading itself out, its structure thinning until it no longer resembled a dragon or even a manta ray, like the *Scintilla.* Now it was becoming a flat surface no thicker than the height of her armor but stretched incredibly wide. The missile launchers and laser mounts that had resembled claws on the ends of its dragon wings were now spread out along its front edge.

The *Über Dragon* had turned itself into something so

vast, it would be difficult if not impossible for two armor jocks and the *Void* to target with any effectiveness. And its black surface still seemed to be flowing ever outward.

Then it began descending toward the ring ship.

Straight toward where Zero's ship had attached itself to the ring ship with the little Alliance ship's tractor beam.

"What the hell did you do?!" Zero screamed over comms. "This is not the cover I had in mind!"

No kidding.

At the rate it was descending, the *Über Dragon* would soon envelope not only Zero's ship but cover the remaining un-gooped portion of the ring ship.

Gus had a good idea what would happen once the ring ship was fully covered in that black stuff. The *Über Dragon* would pull the lasso tight and take off with the ring ship, leaving them all behind.

Except maybe Zero, whose ship would be crushed in the process.

She wasn't about to let that happen.

She needed to throw everything at the *Über Dragon* that she'd thrown at Brukowski to peel the paint off his armor. Only this time she wasn't going to peel paint. She was going to peel skin. And with it, pieces of the *Über Dragon* itself. Or at least enough of the skudging slaver's changing shape to keep Zero's ship free and clear to do what he needed to do.

"Keep this skudge-hole busy," she sent over open comms to both Brukowski and the *Void*. "I have an idea."

She had no idea where the brains were on this thing, and she didn't care. She targeted the part of the Dragon closest to Zero's ship, then powered up her weapons.

Lasers.

Magno-beam.

Projectile weapons.

This was one run that would be do or die.

Brukowski was busy firing repeated bursts of blue lasers from his shoulder-mounted launchers. The Dragon fired back, but its shots went wide as Brukowski easily avoided each one. The *Void* joined in the fight, peppering the Dragon with shots of its own.

The Dragon didn't slow its descent toward the ring ship.

It clearly had one objective in its evil mind, and it was willing to take hit after hit to achieve it.

So let's see how you like getting some of your own skin peeled away, Gus thought savagely.

She kicked in the thrusters on her maneuvering jets.

Her armor shot forward. The leading edge of the flattened Dragon sped past her as she honed in on her target. Blue lasers erupted in space around her, but the Dragon appeared to be channeling the majority of its power into changing its shape as all of these shots went wide as well.

Gus changed her aspect so that when she came out of her roll, her weapons would be aimed directly at the black skin of the *Über Dragon*.

Would this work?

Could she actually carve out a piece of it?

There was only one way to find out.

She heard Brukowski yelling at her over comms, but she tuned him out. Drake was probably cussing up a storm too, but he was smart enough not to interrupt her. She sent a silent prayer his way, then went into her roll.

The targeting system in her armor's visor flashed red as space spun around her.

She couldn't do this by relying on instrumentation.

She had to do this by feel.

She took a steadying breath, and when space turned right side up again, she fired.

CHAPTER 24

The *Golden Void*, from its position at the far edge of the flattened *Über Dragon*, unleashed a complement of mini-drones from a bomb bay on the ship's underside. The drones—a surprise whipped up by Rory—scattered like jacks on the *Über's* glossy ebon surface, then crackled to life with sparking electrical fields…and blew.

All the drones exploded at once, causing a patch of the *Über Dragon's* skin to ripple and change color, shifting from black through all the colors of the spectrum and back to black—but never leaving the vast, thin sheet pitted or torn asunder.

Hopefully, Gus and her team were having better luck. Though Drake had glimpsed the bright white flare of an energy beam near the middle of the *Über's* thin, sheet-like self, he could not yet see if anything had changed.

As he swooped the *Void* across the sheet, strafing it with prolonged energy beam fire, he shouted for the AI's attention. "Still got that spare drone with the bird's-eye view, Bruce?"

"Ten-four, Captain." Bruce was all business in the heat of battle, leaving out the chatter he otherwise tended to engage in. "Putting it on the main viewer now."

Swiveling, Drake saw the main viewer display a high angle shot of the flattened *Über Dragon* above the ring ship's spaceframe. He smiled when he saw the ragged hole where a section of the Dragon's black coating had been burned off, exposing the pale underlayment of a secondary inner surface.

"She did it!" he said. "The Gray Lady just gave us a fighting chance."

"Was there ever any doubt?" Bruce's tone made it clear the question was rhetorical.

A flurry of movement near the Dragon's exposed subsurface caught Drake's attention on the main viewer. "Maximum magnification on the bird's-eye view, Bruce."

The shot zoomed in tight enough to show the team's two armor jocks jetting toward the middle of the field of stripped-down secondary hull. As he watched, they both fired pulses of energy at the pale layer, pounding it with streams of golden force from Gus and blue force from Brukowski.

"What about Agent Zero?" asked Drake. "Show me his current location."

The video feed suddenly changed to a new angle that briefly disoriented Drake...at least until he realized Bruce had cut to another drone under the Dragon. There, in the *Über Dragon*'s shadow, Agent Zero's sleek ship had attached itself to one of the very few spots on the ring ship's hull that was not yet covered in the glossy black Ongoni coating.

"Any update on Zero's progress, Bruce?" he asked. "I can't tell from the visual."

It took a moment for Bruce to respond. "I'm detecting transmissions of executable code from his vessel to the ring ship's control systems, but it's unclear what effect this is having."

Drake pulled a fresh stick of cinnamon gum—the last of the current pack—from his shirt pocket. In the midst of this high-stakes action, he was chewing the stuff like it was going out of style.

"Well, let's see what we can do to keep the slaver off his back," he said.

Punching buttons, checking readouts, and spinning knobs on the nav console, he tweaked the *Void*'s course, then squeezed the trigger on the joystick to engage it.

"Get Gus on the horn, pronto," he said as the *Void* soared over the flat sheet of the *Über Dragon*. "And prep all weapons for immediate activation."

"Gus, ma'am, this is the *Golden Void*," said Bruce. "Captain Mephistopheles would like a word."

"Little busy out here just now, Bruce!" Gus's voice, tense with the stress of battle, crackled over the ship's speakers. "Whatcha need, Broken String?"

"I'm gonna hit that exposed spot on the Dragon's hull," said Drake. "Blow it all the way open."

"I won't look a gift cowboy in the mouth," said Gus. "Brukowski? You copy? We need to get clear."

Brukowski didn't respond over comms, but Drake saw Gus as well as Brukowski in his Ongoni-assisted armor leap up out of the line of fire. That gave Drake all the room he needed.

Chewing the gum furiously, he cut loose with the forward guns and torpedoes, blasting away at the exposed under-layer of the Dragon. As the *Void* raced past, explosions vaulted upward in her wake, ejecting plumes of black smoke and flaming rubble.

Take that, you skudge-hole slaver.

"Another go-round, Captain?" asked Bruce.

Drake was already swinging the *Void* back around and punching the accelerator for all it was worth. "What do *you* think?"

Again, the *Void* charged the *Über Dragon,* pouring magno beams, slugs, and energy beams against her gleaming obsidian hull. This time, though, the Dragon got in a lucky shot, skimming the *Void*'s port side with a sizzling blast of crimson fire that sent the ship spinning.

"Damage report!" said Drake as he fought to regain control of the *Void.*

He had a sick feeling that even the advanced shield generator hadn't been able to withstand the hit. Just how badly had the *Void* been hurt?

"That strike opened a gash in the port hull," said Bruce, "but the protective force fields sealed the tear, and blast doors contained the internal damage. Hull integrity is uncompromised at present, but we can't take another direct hit to the same area."

Drake scowled. The news wasn't promising, and the battle wasn't over.

Be that as it may, he didn't dare shirk the job he still had to do. If the slavers got away with the ring ship, the havoc they could wreak across the galaxy would truly be epic. Damaged or not, the *Void* had to continue manning the front line that yet stood between ultimate power and those Dragon bastards.

"Report noted." Drake's experienced hands swept over the nav controls, changing settings and arming the weapons with what limited ammunition remained. "Prepare for another pass."

"Another one?" Bruce sounded stunned. "But our port hull can't take another direct hit, Captain."

"Which is why we're gonna keep it *facing away* from that slaver skudge-wad," said Drake.

As he started another run at the Dragon, he wondered how much longer Zero needed to finish his work. If Zero wasn't done doing whatever he was doing soon and the *Void* had to drop out of the fight, it would be *game over*.

Glancing at the bird's-eye feed, Drake saw the black coating continuing its advance across the ring ship's hull. Together with the lowering Dragon, the ring ship's surface would be completely covered in a matter of moments. Assuming the slaver would be able to seize control instantaneously or nearly so, time was about to run out in the war to keep the ring ship out of the hands of the Ongoni Dragons.

The thought of the suffering that would surely result was enough to make his heart pound with fresh resolve. It was more than enough to make Drake willing to sacrifice whatever he had to stop the destruction before it began.

Flashing through space, Drake angled the *Void* to keep its starboard hull facing the *Über Dragon* at all times. He focused the shields there, too, and energized the weapons on that side of the ship with the highest possible output.

The *Über Dragon* spat fiery beams from her maw, splashing the *Void*'s starboard hull with a wave of searing flame. Under Drake's swift and confident control, the *Void* shook it off and lit up the *Über Dragon* with a barrage of everything in her arsenal.

Drake pressed the attack, too, pounding away as the *Void* rocked under fire on her headlong course toward the *Über Dragon*. Just before sling-shotting away from the Dragon at the end of her sweep, he fired off another one of the big missiles that had blown up the other Dragon moments ago.

Watching the nav screens as he pulled the *Void* up from her latest pass, his heart sank. The *Über Dragon* dinged the missile with a single precise zap that sent it hurtling off course unexploded.

"The missile missed, Captain," said Bruce, stating the obvious. "And the Dragon's repulsor beam scrambled its guidance system, so we can't bring it back around for a second shot."

"We don't need to," said Drake. "We've got one more missile locked and loaded."

The last big missile in the *Void*'s armory.

The last chance Drake had to do serious damage to the Dragon.

"But what about—" started Bruce.

Drake cut him off. "No buts. We're goin' back in."

This time the enemy's fire was stronger than ever. The slaver belched plume after plume of deadly radioactive flame, accompanied by clusters of energy beams and flights of missiles.

The *Void* danced like a wild fly through this thick bombardment, weaving amid the worst of it while protecting her damaged port side. More energy beam hits glanced off her starboard side, scorching the hull but not quite breaking through. Smart missiles streaked point-blank for her prow, only missing by the scantest of increments.

Perfectly synchronized, Drake and Bruce worked together to push the ship through a field of destructive power that would have seemed impassable to a lesser pilot and craft. They managed to dodge the worst of the assault wave, all while swerving closer to the target and preparing to launch that last big missile.

Just as they were nearly in range, Gus's voice boomed over the bridge speaker. Not every armor jock had a comms override capability built into their gear, but Gus was not just another jock when it came to battlefield comms with the *Void*.

"Get outta there, Broken String!" she shouted. "Move out *stat!* Agent Zero just reported *mission accomplished!"*

Drake felt like letting out a war whoop to end all war whoops. But they weren't out of the woods just yet.

"Roger that, Gray Lady," Drake answered over the open channel. "Breaking away now!"

He jolted the joystick back hard to climb out of the approach vector. He'd get out of there stat, but he had one last thing to do first.

One last weapons button to punch on the way out.

It was a big red button he'd set to fire one item in particular. One piece of heavy armament he'd prepped for just such a close-quarters launch.

The last of the big missiles.

Even as the *Void* soared up and away, he watched the scene he'd set in motion on the main nav viewer. This time the big missile landed square on target, plowing into the belly of the last Dragon and exploding on contact.

The lower front section of the sheeted Dragon burst apart in a storm of sparks and fire. The rest of the Dragon held together, including the flattened head on its elongated neck—but the extreme damage to its bowels left it listing forward in a state of drunken collapse as it fell toward the surface of the ring ship.

Heading directly toward Zero's ship.

Over the open comms channel, Drake heard Gus yelling at Zero to get his ever-loving ass out of there before the injured Dragon fell on him.

For a moment it looked like Zero might make it. His craft leapt away from the ring ship, zipping toward the sliver of open space between it and the falling Dragon.

The little Alliance ship was fast, but it wasn't fast enough.

And the injured Dragon was one malevolent bastard.

As badly hurt as the Dragon was, it still managed to fire a potent energy beam at Zero. The beam slashed open the fleeing ship.

Zero and his ship died in a fireball of exploding energy that was quickly extinguished in the vacuum of space, leaving behind only a multitude of expanding pieces of wreckage.

Drake shook his head, but he had to stay focused on the

next part of the plan. "Get ready to open a transit flume, Bruce."

"On it, Captain."

Holding steady to his course, Drake checked the bird's-eye view of what he'd left behind. As expected, the ring ship was pulsing with bright white light, each pulse coming faster than the one before.

Zero had implanted an override command in the ring ship's system to destabilize the containment field around the singularity. Now that his work was finished, the whole colossal vessel was about to self-destruct. It would implode any minute now, sucking itself and anything around it into a singularity from which not even light could escape.

"Transit flume ready to activate, Captain," said Bruce.

Drake hesitated to give the order to open the flume. Anyone who didn't make it through could never get far enough away by any other means to avoid being consumed by the singularity.

Anyone.

Like two armor jocks.

Like one armor jock in particular.

"Shall I open the flume?" asked Bruce. "We are running out of time, Captain."

"Stand by." *Just one more minute, wait one more minute. Because there's no way I want to live a single day without her.*

"Captain?" Bruce sounded stressed. "Are we going to leave this sector before..."

"Broken String!"

The voice over the speaker unlocked Drake's resolve. "Gray Lady!"

"Brukowski and I are coming aboard!" she said. "Entering the airlock now!"

Drake waited, heart hammering like a fighter's fist in his chest. How long until the singularity devoured this sector? Minutes? Seconds?

Did they even have a chance of getting away before it gulped them down?

If so, at least they would go together.

"Captain?" said Bruce.

"Stand by." Drake glanced at the bird's-eye feed, which showed the ring ship suddenly flaring in its brightest burst of blinding white light yet.

"The singularity's started, Captain!" said Bruce.

Drake didn't answer.

Come on. Come on!

Seconds ticked away with still more silence over the speaker.

Then…

"We're aboard!" shouted Gus. "Go go go go *go!*"

"Open the flume, Bruce!" ordered Drake.

Bruce responded with the kind of speed only a being of artificial intelligence could manage. The flume opened before them, and Drake flew the *Golden Void* straight into it.

The flume closed behind them just as the ring ship finally vanished once and for all and the singularity replaced it, draining spacetime and all it contained in one mighty, inescapable swallow.

CHAPTER 25

Gus stepped out of her armor, powering down each of its systems as she prepared to store it in its spot in the *Void*'s cargo bay. She was drenched in sweat, her muscles ached something fierce, and all her old battle injuries seemed intent on making themselves known. Loudly.

Still, she felt good.

The repairs to the *Void*'s hull were nearly complete. She'd installed the last section of exterior hull plating, with able assistance from Rory and all his multiple appendages. The joys of making repairs in deep space instead of at a space dock.

Drake had agreed with her that they should avoid space docks for the time being. Even in the Frontier, space docks logged the identity of ships that utilized their services. Gus didn't want to take any chances that word of the *Void*'s location and battle damage would make it back to Krepnick. After her last and hopefully final transmission to that particular skudge-hole, she wanted to give him time to cool down and think things through.

She figured that might take a while.

The *Über Dragon* had done a number on the *Void*, but she'd held together. Sort of like Gus herself. She had repairs of her own to do to her armor's weapons systems. Between the last volley of weapons fire from the injured Dragon and the pulsing energy from the ring ship's compromised containment field, portions of the weapons control systems in her armor had shorted out.

Luckily, the controls for her maneuvering jets and the new thrusters that gave those jets an extra kick had survived the battle just fine.

So had Brukowski, although that had been a close call.

In the end, Gus had to clamp onto Brukowski's slower armor to make sure they both got to the *Void* in time and he wasn't left behind to be sucked into the singularity. Squeezing both sets of armor into the *Void*'s airlock made for a tight fit, and she'd had to override the ship's refusal to close the airlock because they'd exceeded the airlock's safety specifications.

But they'd made it. That's all that counted.

Agent Zero hadn't.

He'd been woefully underprepared for the situation he'd found himself in, but he'd provided the only true solution to the ring ship. The code he'd written and uploaded into the ring ship's systems had destroyed the ship, once and for all. No one would be able to use the damn thing to invade territory that didn't belong to them. Not the Ongoni slavers. Not assholes like Jorritz Tor.

Not even Alexander Krepnick.

Current transit flume technology placed limits on the way invading armies could invade. Limits were good things. It kept megalomaniacal assholes more or less in check. Too much power on one side or the other was a bad thing.

Salvagers like Layla Crosscut would be out all that lovely singularium coating the ring ship's hull, but no one would be battling over salvage rights anymore either. Another plus.

Brukowski was gone now. Not dead, just disappeared.

Where he'd decided to go, Gus had no idea, and she didn't want to know.

Bruce had contacted the *Scintilla,* and she'd agreed to transport Brukowski to a place of his choosing.

Not inside the Alliance. He'd said he never wanted to set foot inside Alliance space ever again. As far as everyone in the Alliance knew, Brukowski had died during the battle with Jorritz Tor. He wanted to keep it that way.

He also didn't want to go anywhere near Ongoni space. Brukowski never said what he'd gone through after he'd been "saved" by the Ongoni slavers, but she gathered it wasn't pleasant. He hadn't even wanted to board the *Scintilla* at first until Bruce had assured him that she wouldn't hurt him. She could play a mean game of chess if he wanted something to keep himself occupied during the journey. She'd even play music for him if he wanted.

"None of that cowboy shit," he'd said, "or the deal's off."

No cowboy shit, Bruce had agreed. "She likes rock and roll. The louder the better."

Where Brukowski had ended up was a mystery known

only to the *Scintilla*. Bruce said she would tell him if he ever asked. He also agreed not to ask unless it became absolutely necessary. Gus hoped it wouldn't.

Because Brukowski was her insurance policy.

He was proof positive that the ring ship had existed.

Brukowski might have been a covert operative for military intelligence, but he'd been a *smart* covert operative. The chips he'd installed in his body before he'd left Melody Station on what would be his final assignment for military intelligence had recorded each and every transmission between himself and his handler, the late Agent Zero. They'd also recorded everything Brukowski had done inside the ring ship, which meant they'd recorded the fact that the ring ship had, at one point in time, *existed*.

Brukowski had been surprised that the recordings on his chips had survived his time as a prisoner of the Ongoni slavers. He and Gus had discussed whether that information should be shared with anyone else. Someone like Kymmie, the reporter. But they'd decided that merely having that kind of information would make her a target, and Krepnick would have to disappear her.

"I'm going to disappear myself," Brukowski had told Gus. "Somewhere that Krepnick can't find me. I'd suggest you delete all the information about the ring ship from your AI's memory so that it's not a target too."

Gus wasn't about to do that. Bruce was more than just a ship's AI with a Fluke-enhanced personality. He was a living and more importantly *growing* intelligent entity, and she wasn't going to screw with his brain.

She knew that Drake was concerned that Bruce would outgrow them, but she wasn't worried. Kids grew up. That was just the way of things. Her son had grown into a fine man. She hadn't been around for any of that, and while she had regrets, she'd come to terms with her past. Focusing on regrets meant focusing on the past to the detriment of the present. She had a damn fine present.

And a damn fine man to share her present with.

Drake's voice crackled to life over the cargo bay's speaker.

"You done with repairs for the day?" he asked.

She grinned. She knew where this was headed.

"Well, there's wiring to be done," she said. "Conduits to be installed. Connections to be welded together. I really should get on that."

"Darlin'," he said, "while I appreciate your attention to detail, I think there's one detail you might be over-looking."

She stifled a chuckle. "You're telling me I missed something?"

A chord progression sounded over the speakers. She recognized the song he was strumming on his antique guitar. She should. It was one of Drake's favorites. "Back in the Saddle Again."

"You are missing the fact," he said, "that the honey-moon's not over until I *say* it's over."

Now she did laugh.

"I'm pretty hot and sweaty," she said. "I could use a shower." She paused, then added, "Want to join me?"

He strummed a final chord, then she heard a gentle *thunk* as he put the guitar down.

"Last one in the shower picks up the feathers," he said.

A long, hot shower with her space cowboy followed by

a pillow fight and some definite alone time. That sounded like absolute heaven.

"You're on," she said.

She gave her armor one last pat on the chest plate. She needed to get on those repairs too, but all that could wait.

She *did* have a honeymoon to get back to.

She left the cargo bay at a dead run.

Challenge accepted, Space Cowboy.

Yeehaw!

EPILOGUE

Alexander Krepnick stood gazing out the floor-to-ceiling windows that comprised one entire wall of his office. He had his back to the office, but he wasn't looking at the spectacular view of the capitol city beyond those windows.

He was far too furious to see anything except the message he'd just received through a private link.

If anyone caught a glimpse of him through the clear alloy of his windows, he would have appeared impassive as always. Unflappable. A man in control of his own destiny.

A man to be feared, and for good reason.

As Director of Military Intelligence, Krepnick was the master of secrets. No one dared challenge him. Not the politicians. Not the generals. Not even the rich and famous. No one who'd fought hard to achieve their position within the Alliance would dare risk that position should the secrets he knew about them become common knowledge.

No one.

Except for one lone, retired armor jock.

He'd held a secret over Gus Light's head for decades. She'd fragged a commanding officer. The officer had been an incompetent of no particular importance. She'd probably done the military a favor in the long run, but she didn't have to know that. All she had to know was that Krepnick could release information about what she'd done to the proper authorities, and a military tribunal would bring her up on charges.

There was no statute of limitations on murder, and the murder of a commanding officer was a treasonous offense punishable by death.

So was an attempted coup.

That's what she was threatening him with. Her message had been terse and encrypted with the same code he'd used to communicate with her.

The ring ship is gone for good, she'd sent. *I have incontrovertible evidence that it was constructed pursuant to your direct orders. Evidence that you deliberately withheld knowledge of its existence from the governing council of the Alliance. Evidence that you intended to use it to stage a coup against the Alliance, and that you sent military operatives to their deaths to prevent detection of your treasonous activities.*

That last line had to be speculation on her part. Krepnick *had* sent a junior officer to the far reaches of the Frontier to destroy the ring ship. The assignment would have almost guaranteed the officer's death, but that assignment had never been placed on any official records. In fact, because Krepnick knew the junior officer had been surreptitiously recording their meeting, Krepnick had been careful to indicate that he would reconsider the officer's career path once the assignment was successfully completed.

But the first part?

It was all too true. He *had* ordered the construction of the ring ship, and he hadn't told the governing council of the Alliance or the military, for that matter, that the project was underway.

Krepnick had intended the ring ship to be his crowning achievement. He hadn't built it to facilitate his rise to power within the government of the Alliance. Why should he aspire to a lesser position than the one he already had? He had simply intended to hand it over to the Alliance as a *fait accompli*.

But the mere implication that the ring ship provided him with sufficient power to stage a coup would be enough to ruin him. Careers had been lost over far less than rumors based on suppositions that had only the slightest basis in fact. Politicians already feared him. It wouldn't take much for them to believe he intended to seize control of the government for himself.

For them to turn the tables on him.

Light's message had included a parting shot that set the terms of their détente.

Leave me and mine alone, and you'll never hear from me again.

Nobody dictated terms to *him!*

More than anything else, that last line infuriated him.

Krepnick wanted to kill her.

To hunt her down to the far reaches of the Frontier if that's what it took and destroy her and her partner and the AI that was somehow smarter than any other AI in the

Alliance. To kill her son and *his* son and that meddlesome reporter and every other person who'd ever seen the ring ship or knew about its existence.

But he couldn't.

Most people didn't have the guts to use the secrets they knew to their best advantage. They were too frightened of retribution.

Gus Light wasn't.

She wasn't frightened of anything.

She would carry through on her implied threat to take him down, and Krepnick knew it.

For the first time in his career, his hands were tied. It wasn't a position he was familiar with. If he was a lesser man, he would have torn his office apart just to vent his rage.

But only lesser men would give in to urges like that. To show anger was to show weakness.

He was a patient man. He'd give Light what she wanted, for now. Someday she'd make a mistake. She'd overstep her bounds. Do something she didn't want anyone to know about. Do something she'd be ashamed of.

He'd be right there to remind her that her fate was once again in *his* hands.

He was the master of secrets. Knowledge was power, and that made him the most powerful man in the Alliance. He needed to remember that.

For the first time since he'd received her message, Alexander Krepnick smiled.

It was good to be him.

One day, Gus Light would realize that.

Until then, Krepnick had a job to do.

He signaled his assistant to send in his next visitor. A man whose fate Krepnick would now hold in his hands. A man who'd committed a grievous error he never wanted to come to light. He would be asking Krepnick for a favor. A favor that Krepnick was more than willing to provide.

A favor that would shift the balance of power between them.

The door to his office slid open.

Krepnick turned away from his magnificent view of the capitol city. He pasted a pleasant, benign expression on his face, and held out his hand in greeting.

"Mr. President," he said to his visitor. "What can I do for you on this fine afternoon?"

ABOUT THE AUTHORS

A prolific, versatile, and award-winning writer, **Annie Reed** has written more short fiction than she can count. She's a frequent contributor to both *Pulphouse Fiction Magazine* and *Mystery, Crime and Mayhem*. She's received a Silver Honorable Mention from Writers of the Future, and her stories have appeared in numerous annual year's best mystery volumes. She's even had a story selected for inclusion in study materials for Japanese college entrance exams. Her *Unexpected* series of short-story collections showcase some of her best work.

Her longer works include the superhero origin novel *Faster*, novellas *The Wizard Behind the Curtain* and *In Dreams*, and mystery novels *Pretty Little Horses, Paper Bullets*, and *A Death in Cumberland*.

Annie writes mystery, science fiction, and fantasy under her own name and writes suspense as Kris Sparks. She also writes the sweet romance *Liberty Springs* novels under the name Liz McKnight. She can be found on the web at anniereed.wordpress.com.

***

Robert Jeschonek is an envelope-pushing, *USA Today* bestselling author whose fiction, comics, and non-fiction have been published around the world. His stories have appeared in *Clarkesworld, Galaxy's Edge, StarShipSofa, Pulphouse Fiction Magazine,* and many other publications. He has written official *Star Trek* and *Doctor Who* fiction and has scripted comics for DC, AHOY, and others. His young adult slipstream novel, *My Favorite Band Does Not Exist,* won the Forward National Literature Award and was named one of *Booklist's* Top Ten First Novels for Youth. He also won an International Book Award, a Scribe Award for Best Original Novel, and the grand prize in Pocket Books' Strange New Worlds contest. Visit him online at www.bobscribe.com. You can also find him on Facebook and follow him as @The-Fictioneer on Twitter. Subscribe to the Blastoff Books Newsletter: http://newsletter.blastoffbooks.net/.